Endless

ROY TSCHUDY

authorHOUSE®

AuthorHouse™
1663 Liberty Drive
Bloomington, IN 47403
www.authorhouse.com
Phone: 1 (800) 839-8640

Published by AuthorHouse 01/24/2016

ISBN: 978-1-5246-6851-8 (sc)
ISBN: 978-1-5246-6850-1 (e)

Library of Congress Control Number: 2017900938

Print information available on the last page.

This book is dedicated to all Vietnam veterans.
Our lives do not belong to us, life is a gift.

Acknowledgements

Citing the statement attributed to Dr. Arthur Fletcher, Chair of the United States Commission on Civil Rights.

"A MIND IS A TERRIBLE THING TO WASTE."

The small amount of which I own tries to be of some use. In the end of our physical existence on this earth, anything left with meaning in words or deeds to help guide others is a small gift which should be passed along.

As an active member of Chapter 333 VIETNAM VETERANS OF AMERICA, the meaning of the word 'humility' does not adequately provide due justice. Ours is a group of men who are dedicated in helping not only their fellow veterans, but any others who are in need. It may very well be a natural trait for some folks to seek any which would benefit 'self,' not that this may be bad, as long as that benefit does not arrive at the expense of another.

The principal to "Give Back" as opposed to "What's in it for me" goals is what separates people such as veterans from many others.

V.V.A. Chapter 333 members hold the torch of 'Brotherhood' high, a desire to help veterans in need via resources at hand. Aside from our own personal tithing to charities, Nam veterans of this group adhere to a motto that defines them as a whole; NEVER AGAIN WILL ONE GROUP OF VETERANS ABANDON ANOTHER.

In accordance, this Chapter began a special program in 2013 that would assist returning military IRAQ/ AFGHANISTAN veterans who has suffered wounds leaving them partially immobilized equally on the physical front as well as the emotional aspect. To date, via fundraising along with generous donations from the public and our own members inclusive of MEMBERS OF THE ORDER OF THE PURPLE HEART, Chapter 333 has purchased and donated special HAND CYCLES for two veteran hospitals in the Hudson Valley, five veterans with leg amputations and or spinal cord injury. Additionally, one KAYAK along with a trailer and hitch was purchased and donated to a veteran with disabilities whose preference for open lakes was his choice for rehabilitation and recreation. WHEW!

It should be noted that we maintain certain values which we hold dear,

We hold these principals as truth; we give our time and effort and expect nothing in return for that agenda.

If any who read this book and are aware of a veteran in need of a HAND CYCLE we request that you kindly visit our Chapter website and learn all about us. Please visit, www.vvachapter333.com and learn of the good works us as a group endeavor for. You can also learn of the many other wonderful deeds this particular Chapter is involved with doing.

For instance, the school program that has been set in motion for many years now, presentations made teaching

Middle School along with High School student's personal stories from our time during the Vietnam War. You will also learn that certain Chapter members continually travel back to Vietnam helping the Vietnamese children, orphanages built, medical supplies delivered, schools erected. Not done because Chapter members "HAVE TO," but rather because our members "WANT TO."

Giving back or as the saying goes, "it is better to give than to receive" has never been more appropriate in describing V.V.A. Chapter 333 members.

Thank you for any who purchase this read, please know that each and every penny received from the sale of this book is directed to the aforementioned HAND CYCLE PROGRAM. I further acknowledge this book is as stated a combination of FACT, FICTION, and MYTH. Factual information was arrived from a host of Intel such as WIKIPEDIA, MILITARY SCIENCE FICTION, (www.milsf.com) Vietnam war American Daily News Sheets, United Press International, The DC MAGAZINE, LIFE MAGAZINE, GREEK MYTHOLOGY (WIKI) GERMAN MYTHOLOGY, LATIN MYTHOLOGY, VIRTUAL VIETNAM VETERANS FACES ON THE WALL, AND THE WALL-U.S.A. Memories letters left at the wall.

I further want to acknowledge my Chapter 333 'Brothers' who are good and kind men, in addition to Chapter 333 members, Mitch Serlin Director for Hope for Heroes, Richie Jarco Director for Veteran's Angels, Julianne Williams Director for Woodwill Corporation, Ed Markunas Mayor of Suffern N.Y., Carl Wright Mayor of Sloatsburg, Rockland V.A. Clinic, Jerry Donnellan, Susan Branam,

Lennore & Len Lodico, Rachel Chester, Nina Guidice, Carl C. Dennhardt, Glenn Perrone, Bill Radowick 'YITZ', Ed Day, Alden Wolfe, Greg Cassarella, Marcus and Gene, Phil Tisi, my two ex partners on the N.Y.C. Police Department Kenny McCleod and Richie Corry, my good pal Stewart Zully, my neighbors and friends far many more than I could ever name. The 'Boss' Lois, my children Dawn and Andrew, my Son-In-Law Anthony Vernace, my Grandkids Alexander "THE GREAT," Brandon 'Brando 'and last but not least our newest, youngest to join the team Gabriel.

Not to forget, my little four legged buddies Casey, Abby, and Keifer!

It is not my intent to overlook any who are friends, acquaintances, and relatives; I submit that I truly appreciate all of you who have touched my life.

*Illustration sketch of Tod Moros by Roy Tschudy
* So important I.L.Y.M.B.F.! Roy Boy

CHAPTER 1

ENDLESS

Tod Moros stood there in the dead of night on the battlefield, alone, eyes scanning and searching for what he wanted, the one who's life or lives that he intended to take. Unafraid of injury or any physical harm in the midst of explosions and rifle fire being exchanged between combatants, Tod did not make any movement, no effort to find cover and protection, he just stood there looking…looking.

"Hey Barnett, when we get back to the rear you owe me a beer" chided DuPont, half laughing and half serious. Platoon leader Roger DuPont led a squad of ten young men, members of the 23rd Infantry Division (Americal) stationed near the demilitarized zone (DMZ) in the vicinity of Quang Ngai province.

SP4 Brian Barnett slightly turned his head towards DuPont and stated, "Geez I'd love to buddy, but you know I'm only nineteen and not of age yet. Ha, ha, ha, of course you got that beer and I'll even pay for your next cheap piece of ass to boot!"

In the middle of battle some soldiers can make a little joke or quip to calm the nerves, anything to release the tension, remembering to still stay focused, not dropping your guard down, even a little.

Barnett hunkered down in a small ground opening thanks to an entrenching tool he carried (a small like shovel folded and unfolded) gazing out onto the battlefield lying before him. Squinting his eyes and rubbing away the sweat dripping from his forehead into his baby blues, Barnett could see or thought he could see the solemn lone figure of a man out in the distance, he was just standing there, all alone no movement at all.

Barnett thought about asking Roger DuPont if he could observe the same thing but then thought to himself, nah, my eyes are playing tricks on me. Who or how would any living being just standup in the middle of a dangerous area that exposes their self to injury or death? Barnett kept his mouth shut; don't need or want DuPont and the rest of the guys breaking my balls later on he reasoned.

Ah yes the guys, brothers who are as close if not closer than shared blood in and of itself. They all have been together in Vietnam for seven long months now, one of the previous squad members had completed his year tour and rotated back into civilian life, another was combat injured and medevac'd back to the states for rehabilitation and sadly one big, big loss. K.I.A (Killed in Action) a true hero to his platoon buddies SP4 class James Perrone perished heroically retrieving needed ammunition for his guys. Big Jim was all of nineteen years old in age, six foot four in stature, braved enemy fire which ended while saving the lives of four members in his platoon. James 'Jim' Perrone loved and remembered by all.

This group of young soldiers ranged in age from

nineteen, to the oldest member who is twenty three years old and referred to as 'Gramps' by the rest of the squad members. Lee Pelton, John Palmero, Jon Mash, Jay 'Bird' Fink, Roy Boy Tschudy, Ray Ray, Brian Barnett, Roger DuPont, Bruce Mcclintock, Larry Bensky, Bob 'Gramps' Joyce and the distant member of the squad, by choice, Tod Moros.

Over the months in war along with battles together this squad of young men stood out from other squads of the platoon. They even given a certain nickname "THE NUT GROUP," due to a few of their exploits and antics displayed both during battles and in down time. Although young in the physical sense, each was now much older now, way beyond their years since being placed on this earth. In the inner most thoughts of each was always the notion of their own demise, when alone and feeling disconnected from "The World", (Term described back in the U.S.A.) that singular thought would slowly creep into the mind of how, when, or where he may meet his fate.

Actually one time and one time only did they discuss this among themselves, back in the rear over a couple of beers. 'Death' they shared in a quiet yet poignant way was not only possible but most likely probable. Each one spoke on the subject and each one accepted in their heart and mind of the very real probability. By accepting the idea of probable death, crazy as it sounds, made it easier to function for each one of them.

Hard to explain to people not in a situation called war and it may seem morbid, yet it gave all of them a certain peace along with one less burden to shoulder. In the end, all of us die; it's the timing and nature of how and when.

The irony of war, the irony of combat which leads one to take another's life, even if he is an enemy soldier who also has sworn to take yours, can tear at the soul's core. After all, who is raised to become a person who kills? Each of these soldiers was born and nurtured by loving parents, taught the golden rule, learned respect for others, given principals along with ethics and values to become a decent member of the human race.

During the last year of each of their young lives all of these ideals have been stripped away, war has the ability to take one's morals and flush them down the toilet. Each and every soldier is taught to kill the other guy who is the enemy, kill him in a variety of ways. Trained in weaponry to do the deed, rifle, grenade, bayonet, mortars, hand to hand if need be. Ingrained inside of every person who has become a member of the team is the killing technique; protect your buddies and your own ass at the same time.

When this is finally over and done, when you have been deemed a good soldier, lauded for laying waste to others, each man is now expected to return home and pick up the values he left long ago and resume life as if he was on a vacation, now, now, let's move along shall we?

Scars run deep whether in the physical body or the soul, dreams turn into nightmares; patience is only a virtue for others, no more 'brothers' to protect and none to help protect him. Gone forever is the boyhood pureness once possessed, replaced now with instincts of wariness, cautious of people and possible dangers around…real or imagined. Those who do survive the bitterness of war and battle, who live to a ripe old age, will have the rest of their days defined because of it. Some good and some not so, how you interact with others and how one deports himself.

After an individual has completed their designated service time and returns back to a 'normal' life, personal views have now become emboldened. Witnessing death, destruction, either partaking or observing the debasement of human life, being a member of a team with others who have become akin to blood, never at any time moving forward in life will that soldier allow any to believe they are 'better' or more entitled than he is.

Conversely, walking further down the path of life those who are less fortunate in material ways deserve the same respect of life as all others. Whether ownership, education, affiliations or whatever, we all come into this world the same way and we go out the same way. All of us are equal in God's eyes, make no mistake; those are the only eyes that matter.

Shame on those who believe otherwise because it can be guaranteed they have never supped from the same cup, lent a helping hand or received same, know that if the 'HAVES' found themselves in a time of need with their life dependent upon it, such as in war, they would gladly take the "soiled hand" from a "HAVE NOT" and probably kiss their ass for doing so.

CHAPTER 2

*Lucius Aemilius shifted uneasily on his handsome white stead looking over the battlefield of Cannae Italy; the year is 2 August 216 BC. Both Lucius along with co commander Gaius Terentius Varro are about to engage the Carthaginian military commanded by Hannibal along with his five leaders comprising of allied African, Spanish, and Gaelic tribes. Lucius with Gaius boasted a total strength of a combined 86,400 man army, the Roman infantry 40,000 assisted by 40,000 more allied infantry with 2,400 Roman cavalry and finally another 4,000 allied cavalry, all of them seasoned veterans who have served in many campaigns.

Having their best scouts reporting back to them on the Carthaginian manpower, the contrast in size of warriors between the two armies was heavily in favor of the Roman army. In count total the scouts reported the enemy size was 50,000, heavy infantry owned the most at 32,000 while their light infantry added another 8,000, they did report that the cavalry was large at 10,000. With an advantage of over 36,000 veteran fighting soldiers along with previous historic Roman victory proportions, the battle for Cannae seemed well in hand for Lucius and Gaius.

Tod Moros was a loner, he kept to himself never really

engaging with the other men of the squad. He did not care if others thought of him negatively or what they thought of him for that matter. He kept at a distance from the rest of the squad because that is how he wanted it to be. Tod never offered an explanation for why he always kept his distance from all others nor did he care to do so. He did not bother to try and become a part of the tight knit group of men who considered themselves 'brothers', a stranger in the midst of the men who depended upon each other. Tod Moros knew well one sure thing, he owned a certain and special 'ability.'

Moros always kept calm, never showed emotion to anyone and was self assured in that ability, to snuff out a life with ease. In many ways one could consider him a professional killer, there was no doubt Tod Moros was very good at his job. Whenever a soldier perished in action (K.I.A.) and his remains were returned back to the rear; somehow Tod made sure to be present, watching each and every body bag unloaded. Didn't matter if it was one, three or a dozen, Tod would watch and walk with the stretchers quietly and respectfully, directly into the temporary morgue area setup. Even though Moros was cold and indifferent to others, the dead were treated with his quiet respect. No one ever questioned Tod on this behavior and never addressed it either.

Barnett could not stop thinking about what he thought was 'someone' standing up alone during the last skirmish he and the squad was engaged in the previous night. "I know I'm not nuts" he reasoned, "but I'll be damned if that wasn't a soldier or something weird out there in the field of fire." It was a nagging little thought like someone you recognize from a long time ago but just can't put your finger on their name.

*Both Lucius Aemilius along with Gaius Terentius Varro had been in many battles both as warriors and now commander's of a Roman army. The sword Lucius carries on his right hand side is stained red from the dozens of enemy he has killed in battle, almost smug he is sure of victory. Lucius atop his great white stallion leans forward towards his friend Gaius and asks, "Are you are aware of the unnamed legionnaire in our ranks who lays sway over our enemies in all of our battles, surely you have seen him?"

Gaius has not only seen this certain soldier from afar, he has marveled at the speed and efficiency of this killing machine. "Why has no one brought this valiant soldier before us so we may pay tribute?" asked Gaius. It was agreed between these two commanders of the great Roman Empire that after the victory which surely waits, this special soldier will be properly introduced to them both and feted with platitudes worthy of the gods.

Dressed in full battle gear holding a sword larger than the rest of the other legionnaires as always standing away from the other soldiers preparing to enter battle, Angelus Mortis just stared out onto the battlefield before him, looking and looking. Nothing but cold in his eyes, nothing to say to others, Angelus knew he was about to be a life taker of many that day. As far back as remembered, Angelus was a killer and a very good one at that. Battlefields were left littered with corpses by this mysterious soldier, seen yet unknown by others in the legion.

Angelus was a loner who preferred it that way, if he wanted to make a statement he did so in his own way.

Angelus Mortis was well aware how many times both Lucius Aemilius and Gaius observed him in battle. Only when Angelus decides too, then he will make an introduction to both Lucius and Gaius.

"Chow time!" Tschudy announced to the men, "hot meal boys, gotta get it before it's gone." Just as quickly as Barnett's nagging little thought came, it went just as fast with the idea of hot food. Lee Pelton scoffed the potatoes down in one gulp, "man this beats those World War 2 C-rats in a can for sure." Palmero laughed and reminded the rest of the squad that Pelton comes from the sticks in a rural town named Bardonia, "freakin Pelton eats squirrels for shits sake, and you're complaining about old C-Rations?"

Everyone laughed at that, it was common knowledge Lee Pelton was a hunter who ate whatever he had killed; "Pelton thinks road kill is a delicacy for crying out loud" quipped Bob Joyce as he was rising from his seat and adjusting the belt around his waist. Joyce blessed all the guys with a big wet fart as he stepped out towards the latrine for one of his three a day dumps. Lee Pelton quickly replied to Bob "Don't forget to lick your fingers when you're done taking that crap of yours!" Sharing a hot meal together just as a family, busting each other's balls especially enjoying the two days back in the rear before heading out once again for their next mission. Everyone that is, except Tod Moros.

"O.K. men, start getting your shit together, just received a direct from the C.O. we're heading out early tomorrow" squad leader Roger DuPont informed the team just as they were finishing up what was left of their hot meals. "Any idea where the hell we are headed to this time?" asked P.F.C. Bensky? "Are you shittin me Bensky, why would tomorrow be any different from any others?" "Ah, can't shoot me for wondering" Bensky replied to everyone but no one in particular. Deep long breaths now taken by all. That little thought tucked back in each one of their minds suddenly began to form once again. Specialist Jay "Bird" Fink one of the squads crack riflemen echoed the thought of all the guys, summing it up in one word…SHIT. "Oh yeah, and one more thing, the "Old Man" directed me to make sure it gets done, write a letter home to a family member, friend or whomever you want, if it's the last words they ever hear from you, at least they have that." Fuckin nice thought there DuPont" Mcclintock chimed back. "Nothing like having a positive thought." "Gimme a break and just do it, I don't make the orders, I follow and deliver them" DuPont stated to the group.

"Before I write any letter, I'm gonna try and get a refill on some chow" said Specialist 4th class Jon Mash, "C'mon Ray keep me company." Ray did not have to be asked twice about food, "I'm tight with the mess Sergeant" Ray said. Staff Sergeant Paul Mattern a twenty year veteran in the mess hall department of the Army and Ray Ray came from the same small town of New City located in the hills of Sloatsburg, New York.

"The only problem" Ray warned Mash we most likely are gonna have to sit thru one of Mattern singing one of his ditties". Paul Mattern was a notorious fan of Barber shop quartets and carried that stupid little mouth organ everywhere he went. 'Burrup', "Oh crap, here it comes" Ray said, that unmistakable sound from the tiny harmonica just before a little ditty from Mattern, the price one must pay for a little extra chow.

CHAPTER 3

My Dearest,

How is everything back home honey? Can't wait to see you in just two short weeks for my R&R (Rest and Recuperation) in beautiful Hawaii! That's what I dream about my love, one week in heaven, just you and me. I have the hotel name, the Grand Hawaii on the main land you booked and sent me. The other poor bastards that aren't married are not allowed to get over to Hawaii, only married guys. They do get to go to places like Bangkok, Thailand, Japan and even Australia, from what a few of the guys have said on returning from Thailand, Bangkok is the most appropriately named city in the entire world! Ha, Ha. Gonna get a little shut eye now, nothing happening here in the Nam, it's extremely boring. Write soon, Love ya babe, Bobby.

Bob Joyce Lied.

Dear Mom,

Thanks for the care package you sent, got it the other day and it's almost gone already! Your cookies were demolished in no time, I told you about my buddy Mcclintock Mom, He's not human I swear it! Before the package was even opened Bruce yells out to me "I smell chocolate cookies!!!" Not only that Mom, he even told the squad exactly how many cookies was in the package! Hope Lennore is enjoying her high school year; send me a picture or two of her when she attends her prom. Gonna get some rest now and I'll write again soon. Nothing happening here in the Nam, it's extremely boring. Love Roy

Roy Boy Tschudy Lied.

Dear Ma and Pa,

Miss you and the family much, another four months and a few days from now I'll be back home. Can't wait for some of Ma's home cooking I can almost smell the vittles way over here in Nam. Hey Pa, get the hooks sharpened and start digging up some worms for our fishing trip, don't forget to make up some of your moonshine also!Lot of rain here for the past few weeks, it is now the rainy season. The squad and I are just hanging around here in the camp with not much to do. Sorry to make this short but I'm gonna get a little shut eye now, I will write again very soon. Nothing happening here in the Nam, it's extremely boring. Love, Roger

Roger DuPont Lied.

Yo Frankie,

This is your old pal Sir Lawrence of Bensky writing back to you; sorry it has taken me awhile to do. Glad to hear you are finally getting married, just how thick are your girl's glasses anyway? Joking! Only kidding! Let me know if she has a sister, maybe we can double date but only if she is hot looking. I hope you're keeping the neighborhood in good shape until I get back there, best block in the whole damn city. Selling cars? That's pretty cool man, maybe in the future sometime I'll work with ya, I'm good at B.S.'n and let's face it...that what car salesman do! Nothing happening here in the Nam, it's extremely boring. You're Pal, Larry

Larry Bensky Lied.

Hey Susan,

How's my girl? I miss you and wish I was there to hug and kiss you!!! That pepperoni and crackers you sent was great made me feel like we were back together on Allerton Ave. I shared it with the guys in my squad as we share everything between us. One of the men, Bruce Mcclintock, was eating pieces of the pepperoni between chocolate chip cookies! I can't believe how he can smell food from anywhere and any place. I dream of you all of the time Sue, miss and love you. Do me a favor and check in with my Mom every now and then give her a hug for me and your Mom also! Don't worry about me, nothing happening here in the Nam, it's extremely boring. Love Johnny

John Palmero Lied.

Mom and Dad,

Just received your letter yesterday and as always I was glad to get it. I'm sorry that my letters have been coming later and later, but I guess nothing changes when it comes to the Post Office. What a bunch of lazy bums, they better hope I never decide to work there. Thanks for asking if I want a care package…of course I do! Make sure to throw in a pepperoni and some chocolate cookies, please ask my Jackie to bake them for me she is some great Italian baker! Love her cooking, yum. Going to grab a little sack time now and promise to write again soon. Tell Mom not to worry, nothing happening here in the Nam, it's extremely boring. Love Bruce

Bruce Mcclintock Lied.

Hi Honey Sweetie,

It's the Jay man here front and center! It is HOT here and now it's the rainy season, can't wait to take a real bath. We take these old empty 50 gallon drums that used to have some kind of magic powder which made a jungle disappear in 72 hours, wash it out and use them to take a rain shower. When we get the chance we also do some Bar-B-Quing in them drums, not like home cooking but it will do! Miss you a lot and think of you every day. I'll be home before you know it don't be worrying about me, nothing happening here in the Nam, it's extremely boring. With Love, you're Jaybird.

Jay Fink Lied.

My Dearest Sweetheart,

Hope all is good, just had a little chow with my guys which was pretty good hot food. Sorry to make this short but I can't keep my eyes open! I'm going to turn in for a little sleep and should be fresh as a daisy for tomorrow. Oh yeah, please send me a new pair of good sun glasses, fat ass Barnett accidentally sat on mine and crushed them to bits. Please send a roll or two of real toilet paper, my butt can use a break! Always remember that I love you. Don't worry about me, nothing happening here in the Nam, it's extremely boring. With love, Jon

Jon Mash Lied.

Hi Rona,

Hope all is well with you and your mom, have you been showing off that big engagement ring I got ya? It cost me a pretty penny you know so don't go showing it around because there is always some low life who will want to steal it and then I would have to come home track him down and kill him. Getting married to you will be a dream come true, but even better is thinking how much it means to me to have your mother become my mother-in-law! I love that woman, never a complaint or peep out of her; they should make her a SAINT! May she live to be a hundred and ten or longer! That's it for now; don't worry about me nothing happening in the Nam, it is extremely boring. Love, Brian

P.S. Just got a few stitches in my butt, fat ass Jon Mash left his sunglasses lying around.

Brian Lied, Boy did he ever!

Hello Festus,

What's cookin dude?" I heard our pal Billy Bob won a trophy for 1ˢᵗ place dirt bike racing at the track in Garnerville, give him my best please. Hey, still taking care of my 57 Chevy? I expect a good shine on that baby when I get back home. Is it true they opened a new supermarket around the corner from my house? My brother wrote that on opening day they were giving out free samples of food. When I get back do you think if I tell them I would have been there on opening day but was away in the Nam maybe they can give me some free stuff retroactive? Stay cool dude, nothing happening here in the Nam, it's extremely boring. Your pal, Lee

Lee Pelton Lied.

Hi Everyone,

Our squad was just given a direct order to write a letter home, this is my letter. O.K. for now and will write again soon. Nothing happening here in the Nam, it's extremely boring. Love, Ray

Ray Ray Lied.

Letters now written, folded in half and slipped into a small envelope for delivery back home to friends, and family. Return A.P.O. address neatly printed in the left hand corner, Company, Division, Platoon and Squad, in large printed letters. No need for a stamp, a most fair free benefit for a soldier to be included in war, what sane person wouldn't agree with that exchange!

Standing off to the side observing all the banter and letters being written by the squad, Tod Moros never picked up pen or paper. In truth, Tod did not have anyone to write home to. He was an orphan, without a Mom, Dad or siblings. Moros was a loner and has been ever since he could remember, he preferred it that way.

Chapter 4

*Hannibal ordered his army into a planned double employment or PINCER MOVEMENT, a military maneuver in which forces simultaneously attack both sides of the enemy formation. If you may, visualize the action as the split attacking forces "pinching" the enemy.

The pincer movement typically occurs when opposing forces advance towards the center of an army that responds to the enemy's flanks to surround it. At the same time, a second layer of pincers may attack on the more distant flanks to keep reinforcements from the target units. (Wikipedia BATTLE OF CANNAE)

Dismounting, almost leaping from his large white stead, Lucius Aemilius gazed in disbelief as the battle raged on; the Roman army was being torn to shreds. Standing to the left of Lucius gripping the reigns of his black stallion so tight blood was rushing from the hands of Gaius, the slaughter of the Roman legion before his eyes left him in shock.

The army of Carthage under Hannibal surrounded and defeated the larger army of the Roman Republic, one of the greatest tactical defeats in military history and definitely one of the worst defeats ever leading to the beginning of the demise of the Roman Army. (Wikipedia BATTLE OF CANNAE)

In the end, somewhere between 53,000 and 75,000 Roman soldiers met DEATH, but where was their heroic legionnaire? Lucius and Gaius felt betrayed, how could this special Roman almost god like killer let this happen? Where was our DEATH merchant? Who was our DEATH merchant and why has he not shown himself?

The 23rd Infantry Division (American) is the largest Division operating in South Vietnam with three Light Infantry Brigades along with a squadron of Armored Calvary. The Unit was composed of the 11th, 196th, 198th, Light Infantry Brigades (LIB'S) along with Divisional support units. In addition, Two (2) ARVN Divisions (ARMY OF THE REPUBLIC VIETNAM). The 11th and 198th Brigades were newly formed units. The Division got its start in the rugged terrain of Military 1 then known as TASK FORCE OREGON and was created in Quang Ngai and Quang Tin provinces from the 3rd Brigade of the 25th Infantry Division, and the 196th Light Infantry Brigade all separate Brigades that deployed to Vietnam in 1966.

The Americal was reactivated September 25th 1967 at Chu Lai from a combination of units. Task Force Oregon operated in close cooperation with the 1st Marine Division in the I Corps Military Region. As more United States Army Units arrived in Vietnam the two divisional brigades were released back to their parent organizations and two arriving separate brigades were assigned to TASK FORCE OREGON, which was re-designated as the 23rd Infantry Division (AMERICAL.)

Task Force Oregon operated in close cooperation with

the 1ˢᵗ Marine Division in the I Corps Military Region. As more United States Army Units arrived in Vietnam the two divisional brigades were released back to their parent organizations and two arriving separate brigades were assigned to TASK FORCE OREGON, which was re-designated as the 23ʳᵈ Infantry Division (AMERICAL.)

Thwack! "Crap eatin freakin mosquitoes!" Barnett bitched as he slapped the back of his neck. "Yeah, blood suckers all of them" chimed in Bensky, "I don't know what it is, but I've never been bit one single time by them since I've been in Nam" Bensky continued, both laughing and trying to break balls.

Jay Bird Fink leered over at Bensky and in his best German voice imitation said "Zats becuz ze bug don't like ze Jew! Zay dunt eat, how you say, kosher meat." "Fuck you, you Nazi bastard," Bensky replied, always with the jokes Fink." And by the way, how the hell can you goof on any one, ever, with a screwed up name like F.I.N.K.?" Larry deliberately spelled out each letter for effect. Back and forth it went until each tired of the gamesmanship.

All of the men started to get their gear ready for tomorrow and the operation the rest of the platoon would be embarking on. Not knowing where or what the operation for the next day was nothing new to the platoon, the squad, this particular squad. What they instinctively knew was this was going to be big, really big, and not just another find "Charlie" kill "Charlie" kind of day.

Cleaning weapons, bandoliers of ammo laid out, clean socks stuffed in with all of the other necessary equipment; each member was now quiet and somber, preparing for combat in their own way.

Bobby Joyce always made sure to carry extra water; he often stated the worst part for him out in the jungle for days on end was THIRST. "For me, there is nothing worse than the feeling of thirst in this heat" Joyce continued on to all " trust me boys, I've been there when you can barely breathe and your throat aches for water, leave the extra socks behind in place of another canteen of water, you'll thank me later."The weather in Vietnam is always HOT, add on the humidity fact of which seemed to hover at 100%, the need to hydrate oneself was equally as important for survival as the weapon carried.

Walking back to their tent after that second helping to a hot meal thanks to mess Sergeant Mattern, Jon Mash slowed his pace as he caught something rather odd out of the corner of his eye. "What are you stopping for?" Ray asked quizzically. Out in the dark, just beyond the barbed wire defense perimeter roughly fifty yards away or so, Mash thought it odd that a soldier or a figure of a man would be standing guard.

"Hey Ray, what do you see over there to your right about fifty yards out, just past the perimeter?" "Where?" Ray asked, now a bit bothered to stop for a moment when he needed to get his letter written. "Don't you see that, that guy standing out there all alone, without any other backup?" Ray in his best Mr. Magoo presentation, squinted his eyes until he had a slight headache, "Nope, I see nothing pal, you got "Charlie" on the brain, let's get back to writing those letters. Even with the occasional perimeter camp flares that lit up the area like day time, Ray could not see what Mash had seen… or thought he had seen.

Standing outside the base camp perimeter alone and

silent, Tod Moros stared back at the two soldiers arguing, Jon Mash and Ray. Moros found it neither amusing nor curious that these two friends could not agree what was indeed present. Moros had perfected the art of deception over a long period, it's not that he took pride in this ability to be "unseen" and yet "seen", it was almost like a game for him, akin to being an illusionist.

As sleep slowly began to take hold of Mash lying in his rack, that soldier/figure he thought or imagined outside the perimeter would become his night's bad dream. Ray, fast asleep in his own cot immediately began to dream, his was not a comfortable one. In his dream, Ray could now clearly see what Jon Mash was describing about an hour or so ago. Ray became terrified in his dream, that figure was staring directly at the both of them, Mash and himself. Though the figure in his dream really did not have the shape of a soldier or resemble an innate object like a tree, he was afraid nonetheless.

"For shit's sake, somebody wake Ray up from yelling in his sleep" Palmero complained, "we only have a few hours of sack time left." Too lazy to get up out of his rack, Tschudy threw his boot in Ray's direction, with a loud thud against his leg Ray jumped out from his dream. In unison the rest of the squad directed Ray, "shut the fuck up already!" Ray was secretly happy to be awoken by the boot, he did not go back to sleep again that night.

The rest of the squad members returned to sleep each with a nagging small thought pushing forward in their minds, is tomorrow my time? Collectively yet separately, each young soldier wondered if death would be at the door.

CHAPTER 5

TOP SECRET:

OPERATION: CHAMPAGNE GROVE

QUANG TIN PROVINCE, I CORPS, SOUTH VIETNAM

Location: CHU LAI

Description: The following is an edited version from the American Daily News sheets September xx CHU LAI (AMERICAL IO)-Action remained scattered in the American Division's southern I Corps Tactical Zone yesterday as Division forces and supporting elements accounted for 22 VC killed and one weapon captured. Operation Champagne Grove began on xx Sept in an area 20 miles west of Quang Ngai City. Elements of the 11th Inf. Bde. And 2nd ARVN Div. have killed 110 VC and 13 NVA, detained 27 suspects, captured one crew-served and 14 individual weapon in the combined operations.

Infantrymen of a 1st Bn., 20th Inf. Company two VC who led them to a near tunnel huts nine miles north of

Quang Ngai City. Soon after the two VC entered the tunnel there was a large explosion, killing both VC.

Elements of the 196th Inf. Bde. Killed nine Viet Cong yesterday in the OPERATION WHEELER/WALLOWA area. A recon element of the 4th Bn., 21st Inf. In three separate actions yesterday killed a total of six VC nine miles south of Hoi An. Two 3rd Bn., 21st Inf. Companies killed three more VC in the same area in two separate contacts.

A 5th Bn., 46th Inf. Company found 400 pounds of RICE during a search and clear mission in the Burlington Trail area. The RICE was booby-trapped with two M-26 grenades which were discovered and destroyed.

In other action, a 1st Bn., 6th Infantry Company ran into an unknown size enemy force in bunkers on "rocket ridge" west of Chu Lai. Two air strikes were called in on the NVA unit which was firing on the "REGULARS" with automatic weapons and rolling grenades down a hill into the 1st Bn., 6th Inf. Soldiers positions.

Captain Glenn Riddell was a big man. Not because he graduated first in his class from the West Point Academy, although that's not shabby, the Cap stood 6'4 in height with shoulders as broad as any New York Giant football player ever had. With a booming voice spoken in a staccato sort of way, every swinging dick in Uncle Sam's Army who knew Riddell revered him for his leadership skills.

The "Nut Group Squad" endeared themselves to him for the way they conducted business, "I'm proud of you men" he stated in a semi private area off from the other squads. "I almost feel sorry for the enemy when they encounter you on the battlefield" he stated with a small sadistic grin upon his face. Pointing at Lee Pelton, "soldier, you are quite the end of life machine for Charlie."

It was true; Lee Pelton would sling his M-60 machine gun off of his back in one quick motion and rip out round after round after round, whip another bandolier off his shoulders and lay down spray like he invented it! The squad loved that Lee would have their backs and deeply appreciated him for his special skill sets…much to the chagrin of 'Sir Charles.' Even the loner, Tod Moros grudgingly acknowledged Pelton was good at killing others.

"Another thing I observed out in the field today" continued Riddell, our hardnosed two platoon tunnel rats in Company "C," Spec four William Winter and Sgt. Lombardi kicked some VC butt today. Not only did they take out four VC, they recovered a cache of weapons and managed to bring out two prisoners. I didn't catch the name or rank of the soldier who helped pull the four dead VC from the tunnel opening but he worked fast and proficient. I'd like to thank him personally also if any of you can get me his info. Damn good work, hot damn!"

Tod Moros did not need the Captains thanks and did not want his approval, Moros just being Moros.

Ray Ray was the last man to join the squad, before him, Private E-2 Cliff Fromm was a main fixture in the "Nut Group". The Cliffster as he was known would crack jokes nonstop. The squad could be in a fierce fire fight, ammo running dangerously low and Cliffster would lean over to whoever was next to him and say, "Did I ever tell you about the one…" Unbelievable! It did not matter to Fromm if his joke was corny or not, like a dog has to scratch a flea, the Cliffster had to tell a funny anytime the mood would strike him.

During one such incident in the throes of a later firefight, tensions mounting high, music playing from the movie "HIGH NOON" in the ears of his buddies as the shit was hitting the fan, Cliffster leans over and begins "Did I ever" the following word never had the chance to get out of his mouth. An enemy round found its path directly into Cliffster, smack dead into his ass!

The platoon's medic was a "GOODMAN", affectionately called Theodore by everyone in the platoon just because they all knew he hated that name and wished only to be called Ted. Looking at the gaping hole in the Cliffster's derriere Ted Goodman the medic stated, "I always thought you were talking out of your ass, now by the way things look, you'll have twice as much to say!" Goodbye Cliffster, hello Ray Ray.

February 1968-The 1/14th infantry and 1/35th infantry (3rdBde/4th infantry Division attached to the 23rd infantry Division) meet the 21st NVA Regiment near Go Noi island, 12 miles south of Da Nang. More than 230 of the enemy are K.I.A.

Comment: WHEELER/WALLOWA is a combination of the 1st Calvary's Wallowa (October x – November x) and the 23rd infantry Division's Wheeler (September x-November X). Casualties: U.S.-682 K.I.A. 3,995 W.I.A.; NVA/VC-10,008 K.I.A. 184 POW'S.

Death can arrive at any time, any place and to anyone stationed in a designated war zone. The entire country of Vietnam was a damn war zone; there is not any dispute that the chance of becoming a statistic is far greater to some with a different M.O.S. than another. However, death decides who will be taken, when and where it chooses to do so. Firefights, rocket and mortar attacks slamming down near and around any soldier can seem ENDLESS, even if in reality they may last only for a short time. Battlefields are not necessarily just an area where combatants from both sides shoot at one another. Men have met their doom in 'the rear' on bases and compounds alike. There really is no 'Safe' place, less dangerous yes, but the arm of death can reach out and touch any in a war zone.

Death lurks in all places, it is not biased against a soldier's race or religion, and it could care less if a soldier is short or tall, young or older. Death has only one job to do and it is extremely good at doing it. Before it grabs a hold of the soldier do you think it whispers in his ear? Does he introduce himself in a way that cannot be imagined? From the beginning of man throughout the ages, Death prowls places of war anywhere, and everywhere.

Death has many faces and many names, it comes as one yet it also comes as many. War Death is found in all areas when men and countries decide it has nothing better to do, when the gift of life and regard for others has little or no value. "Everyday Death" has its own job to perform and is also just as efficient as its brother, War Death. Everyday death is busy taking life from cancer to car accidents and just about everything else in between.

War Death is different; it chooses who it will take from a battlefield and who it decides to pass by. Make no mistake, any who have heard a shot fired in anger during war inherently is aware War Death was near. Any who survive battles and skirmishes, survived pitfalls and all which is associated with war, each carry down deep in their soul for the rest of days, the knowledge for whatever reason, War Death decided to pass them over.

Tod Moros was acutely aware of this; Tod fully understands that both LIFE and DEATH are the same equal partners in God's plan. The difference between these two partners'? LIFE is short, DEATH IS ENDLESS. This special squad of soldiers also knew and accepted this, they just did not understand the depth of it the same way Moros did. War Death decided to work "overtime" one week in late Spring May 28 through June 3rd 1969. Death is unforgiving in war, in that one weeks period of time it took 243 American military souls with it. Vietnam, yeah this has been a nice cozy little place for the taker of life, taking from both sides of War Death's tournament.

CHAPTER 6

LIFE MAGAZINE published the photos of American dead for that week in the June 27th 1969 edition, 242 pair of eyes staring directly back at the reader. Find a moment if you will, take a look back at the photos of those lost lives, and still after these many years, frozen in time for all of eternity, those very same set of eyes, the same 242 war dead remain staring back at...'YOU.' ENDLESS, ever ENDLESS.

On a clear summer's day if you happen upon a small pond or lake, bend down and fetch a small stone. Now toss that stone upon the water and observe the ripples spread wide and wider. The effect from ONE stone creates MANY small waves. When DEATH takes the life of ONE soldier, the ripple effect of grief creates many waves as well. Family, friends, acquaintances and even those unknown to the one who had made the ultimate sacrifice, are emotionally hurt by his loss.

Death is a Bitch.

Sitting around back at base camp one day cleaning weapons doing the usual check list on items needed for patrol and also doing what each does best... bust balls and bullshit. "Mcclintock looks over at Brian Barnett who is threading a needle to sew a hole in his sock where the big toe protrudes out similar to a turtle sticking its head from a shell.

"So Barnet," Mcclintock begins, "What do you plan on doing when you get out of the Army?" As the sharp needle finds its way through the hole in the raggedy sock belonging to Barnett, it also enters his right thumb emitting a squeal that the others find hilarious. "One thing for sure" laughed John Palmero, "he ain't gonna be no Haberdasher!" "Open a PLUM FARM" Barnett answered while sucking the little blood droplets from his thumb.

"Plum Farm?" everyone queried in unison, "Let me get this straight, you're gonna grow PLUMS for a living?" Mash half questioned, half in shock answered back. The opening for ball busting was presented unwittingly by Barnett and he now braced himself for the onslaught he knew was about to come. "Well, I would like to own a nice Jewish Deli one day" Bensky said ignoring a chance to bust them on Barnett. It would take a lot of money to do, plus I would need to find a good location for it to work.

A good location would be Tel Aviv Jaybird Fink replied laughing at his own humor, Bensky said "I'm not even answering you bird." "O.K. I get it, and really honestly hope that you do" replied Jaybird in a moment of sincerity. Instead of busting chops on Barnett for his future job desires, each of the squad began to offer up what they hoped for back in the world.

John Palmero offered that he has always been good in the subject of math and guessed that his future could possibly be in banking or something with a numbers crunching department. There was not any doubt among the squad that Palmero was sharp, if he said he wanted to get a job in anything to do with adding and subtraction they knew his future would be a success.

Roy Boy countered he had absolutely no idea what kind of career was in his future. He doubted higher education would be part of his hopes knowing his lack of study habits was bare bones. The desire deep down to become a professional baseball player remained Roy Boy's real dream. Never the student athlete, just the athlete, sports always came easy and natural to him. During basic training at Fort Jackson South Carolina when it was time for the final P.T. exam, Tschudy came in second place in the entire Brigade. A final score of 498 out of a possible perfect 500, the kid in his haste slipped on the parallel bars and fell to the ground attempting his turnaround. Roy Boy had no other plans for his future career.

"My Uncle is a plumber with his own business," interjected our squad leader Roger DuPont. "He told me that I can apprentice under him if I want, and eventually become his partner or even own the business one day." Jon Mash thought that DuPont had a terrific chance at his plan, "I'm gonna take every single civil service test in New York City that is available when I return home" Mash announced. "I'll even become a freakin sanitation man if I pass the test, those guys make big bucks with all of the O.T. they get."

Now, everyone in the squad was on a roll, really interested in each other's aspirations. As per the course and as usual, Tod Moros stood off to the side in a corner alone from the other's listening to the men talk about life after war. Never saying a word of encouragement, never engaging in the ball breaking antics that made them a small family, the strange existence of Moros with the squad continued, he was treated like he wasn't even there.

"Fireman!" "That's what I always wanted to be since I was a little kid" Jaybird Fink said passionately. Well admittedly, actually I would rather be a Cop, but if that doesn't work out for me then I would take the job as a smoke eater. The test to become an officer is pretty hard from where I come from, fireman test is easy.

"What about you Ray?" Bobby Joyce was really into this now, enjoying the camaraderie of the team."Haven't had a lot of thought on it, I think schooling may be best to start out with."Ray replied. I'm not thinking that far ahead to tell you the truth, just concentrating on surviving one day at a time." Hearing what Ray said, Moros began to reply… then decided not to.

"Ya know, I've been thinking a lot about a certain job lately that I never considered before" blurted Bruce Mcclintock. Before any of the squad could ask what kind of job Bruce was thinking about, he blurted out "THE POST OFFICE!" I have become one pissed off soldier with a rifle and I'm mad as hell. We send letters home and they arrive whenever, I know that I am qualified for the job based solely on my kill ratio. Another thing, if they can hire David Berkowitz who is my neighbor Sam's kid, they sure as heck can hire me! He is one strange dude." For the first time since being attached to the squad, Tod Moros smiled…then slipped out of the tent unnoticed.

How to explain Lee Pelton to anyone who did not know him borders on the impossible. In the middle of Vietnam in the rear area where the troops can rest a little before heading back out into the jungle, Lee saunters into the tent area licking an ice cream cone! "Where in God's good earth did you get an ice cream cone?" Jon Mash incredulously asked. "Not telling," was the reply from Lee. All of the squad was looking at Pelton and his now dripping cone, "Pelton! Where did you get the ice cream? Ray asked also, more forcefully than Mash.

"Awright awready, got it from the ice cream truck rolling around the compound" Lee finally answered. All of the squad sat there not knowing what to say next, too dumbfounded to ask another question. Lee shrugged his shoulders as if it was just another day at the park and walked out of the tent licking his sticky fingers on the way. Later that night upon learning that the guy's were telling each other about their future hopes and plans, Pelton told all of them when he gets back to his hometown a job with O&R (Orange and Rockland Utilities) was his. He already took the test and was already accepted, freakin Pelton.

With a touch of an Irish brogue in his voice "My family has been working on the DOCKS of NEW YAWK since the Irish were allowed to have jobs" Bob Joyce bragged. The 'guineas' think they own the area but we 'micks' are the real boss of the waterways. My grandfather and my pop have worked their asses loading and off loading everything from cars to furniture to booze! And that my friends, is where I will be making my fortune, oops, I mean my living. Ha, ha, and yadda da da! With that Bobby Joyce performed a little jig.

A directive from HQ was sent down to all squads with a reminder on all "Search and Destroy" missions for squads to be attentive for enemy Booby Traps. Over the last month, an inordinate amount of K.I.A. (Killed in Action) and W.I.A. (Wounded in Action) was reported due to said condition. An example illustrated pencil drawing attached to the directive described a small well covered three foot pit containing sharp bamboo Punji sticks. Each sharp stick end was covered with both blood and feces; the intent was meaningful in a multitude of ways. First the enemy set the trap to seriously wound an unsuspecting soldier who happened upon it, secondly, kill him. A combination of blood and feces would most likely inject infectious disease disabling that G.I. Any others attending to aid their injured comrade would become subject to an ambush with the real possibility of taking the entire squad out.

Ingenious little fuckers those V.C.

Early that day a conversation between platoon squads was led by the two designated tunnel rats, Sergeant Anthony Lombardi an already highly decorated soldier and his partner SP4 William Winter also highly decorated in his own right. Physically both men were ideal candidates to perform a job function that required bravery above and beyond, the best way to describe these two and all others who would enter the enemy's unknown dark lair is THEY GOT SOME SET OF BRASS BALLS!

Winter was 5"6 in height and 110 pounds soaking wet, explained that his preference entering a tunnel was to be armed with a knife and ONLY a knife. Pulling out the blade from the sheath attached to his belt, William Winter displayed a special homemade designed kill weapon. In awe, Bob Joyce mused aloud "Oh man, that blade could cut the ears off of an elephant." Squad leader Roger DuPont looked over at Joyce and replied, "It may do just that but the real test would be if that blade could cut off one of YOUR

EARS!" Everyone cracked up, Bob Joyce God love him, possessed ears that would make 'DUMBO' proud. Joyce could only retort with the obligatory… "FUCK YOU."

"I don't use a flash light that would be a dead giveaway pardon the pun" Winter continued, a .45 cal would be of no use unless I would care to become completely deaf. With the blade glistening from the hot sun which was ever present, William Winter stood up and with three quick moves in the blink of an eye, showed all in attendance his kill technique. Thrust, stab, slice, and see ya in the next life.

Any Viet Cong who had the misfortune of engaging Will Winter in the darkness of a tunnel had their fate met then and there. The blade held tight in the hand, caressed and loved same as a new born by its mother was returned to the sheath in one smooth motion.

Sergeant Tony, as he was known by the platoon members, was equally adept at seeking the enemy, finding him/her, killing or capturing him/her. Lombardi measured 5'4 in height and also weighed in at about 110 pounds. Every single one of the 110 pounds was mean and ornery."Tunnel darkness is unlike any other darkness" Tony went on. Even on a dark cloudless night there is some sort of light, street lamps, car lights, or simple reflections are just a few examples he explained. Inside the tunnels is absolute darkness, the absence of light, essentially you are blind. The need to rely on other senses such as smell, hearing and touch is the difference between you staying in that tunnel as rat food or emerging out, alive.

Is it any wonder why these two highly decorated soldiers had earned the admiration and respect from their 'brothers'? A fact that should not be lost on any, a tunnel rat's job was deadly for both the enemy and the soldier. Out of every ten who dared enter into the lair of the Viet Cong, statistics show only five came out, 50% were either successful… or not.

Tod Moros always found ways to stay busy and never seemed perplexed at or concerned when orders were directed to the platoon for missions and especially for the "Nut Group Squad." After slipping unnoticed out from the tent while Mcclintock and the rest of the squad were engaged in their future hopes, Tod decided to make a quick visit beyond the camp perimeter.

CHAPTER 7

Approximately one hundred meters out in the dense jungle coverage, two North Vietnamese soldiers (N.V.A.) quietly sat observing the American base camp. Nguyen Chi Tho and Vo Van Than was part of a scout team for a North Vietnamese Regiment located three miles to the north. Their job was to gather as much information as possible regarding the size of the camp, troop movements, positions, along with anything else deemed vital.

The order of "not to engage the Americans" was understood by both long time combatants. They were both Hard Core, been in many battles with the Americans and their allies. Trusted to this mission by their commander Tran Van Tra, the planned attack to overrun this particular base was important both for strategic reasons and to help promote the division that was now rampant in the United States between protesters and Washington D.C.

"Uncle Ho," as he was lovingly referred to by all in the north of Vietnam was still regaling in the recent visit of the American actress Jane Fonda. Ho Chi Minh was the Communist revolutionary leader who was prime minister and president of the Democratic Republic of Vietnam. "Hanoi Jane" as she has become referred by received an invitation from the North Vietnamese president to visit the famous Hoa Lo Prison in Hanoi, A.K.A. "THE HANOI HILTON."

This anti war protestor and daughter of famed and respected actor Henry Fonda, gleefully posed for a photo-op sitting atop of a North Vietnamese anti-artillery weapon "Hanoi Jane" envisioned herself as this great humanitarian, someone who would prove to the world how the big bad Americans bombed, killed, and destroyed a kind and peaceful people. Grudgingly appearing in photos with captured American pilots, copilots, and navigators, the now traitor Jane Fonda reported to the world in all of herself righteous statesmanship that the American prisoners are being treated with respect, are well fed and cared for. She must have reasoned in her twisted small mind that her actions would be taken as Bible verse, after all who would ever challenge a great actress with acclaim to a movie starred in as "BARBARELLA!"

Ngyuen Chi Tho and VO Van Than froze in their positions neither could move and both were speechless. As quickly as an unexpected breeze appears out of nowhere on a brutally hot day, Tod Moros swiftly approached both soldiers out of the darkness. In that second both N.V.A. soldiers became acutely aware their mission had failed. Observing the deed, Moros watched as the last breath of life escaped each of their lives. Tod Moros turned quietly and headed back to base camp.

Resting on the makeshift bed belonging to squad leader Roger DuPont was a letter, it was addressed: TO THE NUT SQUAD, quickly looking at the return address at the top it simply said THE CLIFFSTER. DuPont smiled

to himself and said out loud, ARE YOU SHITTIN ME?'
Later that day DuPont and the rest of the squad sat down
with John Palmero reading the newly received letter out
loud to all. It began; Hello My Squad Brothers! I hope all
of you are doing good and ducking fire better than I did,
Ha, ha. Still having a little trouble sitting down and forget
about taking a dump, oy vay. Geez, how will I ever tell my
grandchildren their old Pop got shot in the ass during the
war? I have a few years before I think of a good story but
you know me, it will be a doosie.

Who would ever believe that taking a round in the
ass would bring good luck, not me that's for sure. Then it
happened, I met a beautiful and gorgeous nurse who tended
my wound with the hands of an Angel, her name is Marilyn.
Marilyn has taken such good care of me and has seen my ass
now more than I even have! Then again it's not easy to see
your own ass unless you have a mirror and why would I want
to see my ass in the first place? I don't know whatever. Well
I just proposed to Marilyn and she accepted, this turned out
to be a great trade, a bullet for a beautiful lady! Write back
when you guys get a chance, remember to stay low and don't
take any stupid chances. Your pal, Cliffster.

P.S. As luck would have it, we are both of the same faith,
she's a Lutheran also! What Cliff Fromm decided not to add
in his letter to the squad was just prior to getting hit Cliff
saw a vaguely familiar figure, someone or something he has
seen many times in and around the squad. Cliff could see
and yet could not see at the same time, but he could "feel"
it right next to him, can't put my finger on it.

As Cliff Fromm sat and remembered that moment
in time, a quick chill passed directly through him, an

unmistakable chill different from others. Jokes are one thing Cliff loved; having his pals think he was loony was quite another.

Death whispered into a soldier's soul,

"I am here, do not fear me, nor fear not my touch. Gaze upon me as I take your hand and lead you home. Watching you on the field of battle I have stood still and quiet, waiting, waiting. You know me; you have seen me from afar and wondered. Wonder no more."

Roy Boy started laughing to himself, "Hey Jaybird, remember the time back in Can Tho when the squad had a day to ourselves and we went to that bar in town, Noh Bai Bak?" The Bird remembered and was not happy about it, "nah, don't recall it" he replied. "Who are you bullshittin?" Tschudy replied, you're trying that old selective memory again, you freakin remember my friend, you remember."

The squad sat in a little strip club in the Can Tho area about 70 miles south of Saigon located in the Mekong Delta. Enjoying themselves with a few beers, this one particular very pretty Vietnamese Baby-san had latched onto the Jaybird and had him buy her about six or seven Saigon Tea's. "You number '1' Jaybird" she would tell him and hug him after every tea he would buy her. "Two dollah please" only MPC no Piaster's" as another tea was set down for the young lady. (Military Payment Currency) (Piaster's, Vietnamese Currency)

Jaybird was of the belief that this was his "LUCKY NIGHT." And It just may have been only if…if a young handsome blonde Buck Sergeant who also possessed the physique of a chiseled god had not entered the Noh Bai Bak Bar. Looking at the name stitched over his breast pocket, 'RADOWICK' in black lettering, walked up to the bar and spoke quietly into the bartender's ear. Baby-san with her mouth agape and eyes as wide as moon beams turned to the Jaybird and said, "You no good, you number '10,' bye, bye."

In less than TWO MINUTES Buck Sergeant RADOWICK was walking out of the door with little miss Baby-san on his arm. "Fucked again" Jay stated, "No, you mean ALMOST FUCKED!" Larry Bensky replied, laughing and thanking Tschudy for bringing back a wonderful memory.

"Hit the deck boys, we're heading out for work" Squad leader Roger DuPont speaking in a loud and disciplined voice yelled to the squad. In truth, each member of this special squad had been awake for over an hour each preparing his gear and own mental status for the mission, OPERATION CHAMPAGNE GROVE.

With the entire platoon in place along with the other support groups, Father Kenneth McCleod stood before the men and offered up a prayer to the Lord for blessings and protection. "God be with you my children, have faith in the Lord" with his right hand held high making the sign of the cross."Does this mean I'm screwed whispered Bensky over to Jaybird Fink? Jay calmly reached out placing his hand on Bensky's left shoulder with full sincerity said "Not today my friend we'll be fine don't worry." This caught Bensky a little off guard but then he remembered, ball busting and real compassion shared among each of the members in the squad rose above all else.

Thump, thump, thump, the blades of the "slick" UH-1

Huey Gunship rotated above the heads of the nut group squad as they scrambled out to a clearing. "Mcclintock, take point" squad leader DuPont directed, in actuality it really didn't have to be ordered, Mcclintock always walked point on patrol. Not only did Bruce himself want it that way, the rest of the squad trusted him for that job.

Bruce Mcclintock recently had his twentieth birthday in the Nam and celebrated the day with his squad "brothers". Bruce felt a lot older than twenty years old, a hellava lot older. Mcclintock was born with an uncanny sense of smell, from early childhood Bruce could smell the difference between a winter's snowflake and the air in between each flake. The sense of SMELL was a huge part of his D.N.A. which could put a hound dog to shame, as all in the squad would attest whenever a care package from home would arrive.

This special squad who have banded and bonded together for months are well prepared for patrol, a function that is engrained in them as a team. A fire team is a small military sub-subunit of infantry designed to optimize "over watch" along with fire and movement tactics in combat. Depending on mission requirements, a typical fire team was made up of four (4) members; an assistant automatic rifleman, an automatic rifleman, a rifleman, and the designated team leader. The job of each fire team leader is to ensure the fire team operates as a cohesive unit. In coordinated operations two or three fire teams are organized into a squad or a section led by a squad leader.

All patrols have one thing in common.

They must go into a combat zone.

Avoid getting lost while in it.

Get out of the combat zone without getting shot.

Using a zig zag line to travel the patrol route mapped out for them, the squad moves out with Mcclintock at point, followed by Roger DuPont, Lee Pelton, Roy Boy, Bensky, Ray Ray, Mash, Jaybird, Bob Joyce, and Barnett. Moros was always in the rear watching the squad in front of him, just as the squad preferred McClintock to walk point, Tod Moros made sure to always trail behind the rest.

The sun broke thru the thick jungle in slivers of ray beams, hot and humid as always they pressed on paying no mind to it. Concentration levels coupled with skills honed over many patrols things that would physically impact the everyday person was just a normal part of life for these soldiers, this squad.

DuPont raised his right arm after a nod from Bruce Mcclintock for the squad to halt, for thirty long seconds there was not any movement just silence. Roger signaled to the squad to take five for a small rest and take a swig from their canteens filled with water. This was most appreciated by Bobby Joyce who could feel that ever familiar tightening of dryness in his throat.

Tschudy whispered over to John Palmero "Glad I put that grape Kool-Aid into the canteen, water here takes like shitty metal in your mouth," and with a nod towards the sky, said "thank you mommy." Roy Boy was speaking truth, to avoid coming down with the shits all military personnel put two iodine tablets into their canteen of water for purification. Doing so made the water taste metallic, many soldiers writing home requested Kool-Aid to add a little taste.

This squad of young men possessed the two most needed requirements during patrol, discipline and common sense. The nut group squad has been together for months and each knew and trusted the two aforementioned abilities as a team.

There have been times when a patrol came under enemy fire from artillery and or mortars and a patrol leader gave the order for everyone to break up and make their way back to a designated rally point. That would never be the case with this particular squad of 'brothers,' if that order was ever to be directed for them, you can bet sure as shit it would not go down, to hell with the consequences.

CHAPTER 8

Bob Joyce held his canteen high for one last long swig of water, Zzzst! zzzzst, zzzst, zzzst enemy rounds knocked the canteen from his hand landing in front of him. "Take cover!" DuPont screamed, in that five minute break 'Charlie' had the squad surrounded in the jungle canopy. Pelton readied his M-60 in a split second and began spraying round after round into the dense jungle area. The battle was on, no thoughts of home or girlfriends, not bothered by heat and insects, only what was in front or behind them mattered.

The squad did not have knowledge of the amount of enemy troops, Viet Cong or North Vietnamese regular army, what they did know from past skirmishes was a ton of fire power was being directed upon them. Thirty seconds after the attack began...all stopped, nothing but silence with the panting of heavy breath escaping their mouths. The thirty fifth second was different, the loud BLARE from a horn immediately let the squad know this was an N.V.A. attack with a human wave assault on the way.

Instinctively the squad began to fix bayonets to their weapons, Larry Bensky did not have a chance to take aim, he whirled and fired his M-16 in one motion dropping the charging enemy soldier at his feet. And then they came hot and heavy at the squad, so many like ants streaming from their little mound of dirt. Ray, called for backup on the radio he was designated to carry, giving the squads coordinates at the same time squeezing off rounds flipping the small switch from semi-automatic to full automatic on his M16 rifle.

This squad, this special squad of young men fought like heroes of the past, brave and valiant each cared more for the life of his 'brother' than his own. Those who like a good old fashion war movie on television or at a Cineplex enjoy a certain advantage. When the show is over they either are home or leave to get there. Commercial break means a fast move to the fridge or the bathroom, popcorn by the handful and a "wow" here and there.

For Mcclintock, DuPont, Joyce, Fink, Tschudy, Ray, Bensky, Palmero, Pelton and Mash there were none of those luxuries. Adrenalin flowing to the highest degree possible, focused on the matter at hand to the umpteenth degree, survival instincts taught and those which are inherent automatically settle in.

As many times these men have tasted combat, make no mistake, fear is also a part of that process. The fear component can drive the combat soldier to perform in ways that he never imagined because survival instincts compel him to kill before he can be killed. It is suggested, all who have been in a situation of finality of life is scared at one point or another.

Smack dab right in the middle of all of this chaos and killing, Tod Moros was front and center. Moros never came close to breaking a sweat as many N.V.A. soldier's soon discovered while trying to annihilate the squad. In unmatched efficiency, Tod methodically dropped one N.V.A. after another. Not one other squad member or platoon member could snatch out a life like Tod Moros could; he was that good at his job.

Every member of the squad was killing in his own way, killing the enemy as fast as possible, yet at the same time each was aware of the position of their 'brother.' It is almost uncanny how many thoughts can enter the human mind at the same time and then process what is needed at that moment.

The smell of DEATH hung heavy in the air, dead and dying enemy littering the small trail pass where the squad had stopped for a small rest, the drink from a canteen that seemed like a hundred years ago yet was only twenty minutes in the past. Slinking away in the fading daylight back into the thickness of the deep green jungle, the enemy returned to parts unknown. Jaybird with blood streaking down both arms from his kills screamed back at the fleeing enemy, "Anytime, anywhere you bastards, you messed with the WRONG SQUAD" he bellowed loud and clear, ' Xin Loi!' (Sorry about that) In the near distance as his troops were retreating back into the jungle, Commander Phan Xuan Giang could hear Jay Fink's words, silently admiring the fighting spirit of the American, and then thought to himself "they don't understand yet, but they will eventually most certainly lose."

"Medic!" Jon Mash screamed out while cradling Bob Joyce in his arms, Bobby received a bayonet wound into his right side through and through, "fuck that cock sucka, I killed that son of a bitch that motherfucka" Joyce was delusional, ranting. You killed him good Bobby, relax now your gonna be fine pal." Ted Goodman applied direct pressure to the wound stopping the gushing blood loss. "I'm giving you a shot of morphine for the pain" Ted explained, "Stick that up your ass Theodore, just give me a shot of Johnny Walker and a band-aid. Ted smiled and slowly shook his head looking down at Joyce replying "It's Ted you big asshole" sticking the plunger into Bobby's leg with a shot of happy juice.

Every squad member had wounds from the engagement, some small and others a bit more. Was it a miracle, divine intervention, luck, skill, or training that not one of the team belonging to the nut squad perished? The chance of survival for an entire squad who has been attacked from a much larger force is almost unfathomable, yet there the squad stood albeit bloodied but still unbowed. In the stillness of the aftermath, while waiting for a helicopter back to base camp, the battle area became a photo-op in the minds of the squad.

Hardened hearts, hardened souls, older than their time even more so than earlier that morning, and always acutely aware that DEATH is their constant companion.

During that ambush by the North Vietnamese regulars the squad learned one of the squad's favorite platoon Sergeants also was wounded in action. Sergeant Howard Goldin highly regarded by all who knew him took four enemy rounds to his right leg It also was not surprising to learn Howie was instrumental in forming his squad into a specially designed maneuver, outflanking the enemy combatants inflicting heavy damage and surprising an enemy who believed they were surprising him and his troops. That is one shit load of surprising!

As Goldin was lying on a stretcher and being put into a medivac helicopter, he yelled back out to his men, "Be back in a month, hold down the fort!" They don't make too many like Howard.

In the flash of an eye, twenty three year old Warrant Officer John Leighton lifted the wounded aboard the helicopter 'slick' streaking back to a safe zone and medical attention for the wounded soldiers. Leighton was a fearless young pilot who volunteered to fly many sorties in the face of any danger. Soldiers could spot Mr. Leighton's 'Bird' from far away, always adorned with large lettering of the N.Y. Yankee's logo on the left side and an American flag in very large wording "VOTE REPUBLICAN" on the 'RIGHT' side.

"Yea though I walk through the valley of death I will fear no evil, because I am the meanest son-of- a-bitch in the valley!" Or so the soldiers' saying goes.

Three weeks and one day after the battle of OPERATION CHAMPAGNE GROVE the squad received a happy and pleasant surprise. Poking his head thru the tent flap opening one ear at a time, Bobby Joyce with a twinkle in his eye along with a broad smile announced to the squad "I bet you didn't think for a moment I'd be back?" 'Joyce!' all of the squad members screamed out loudly in unison, each man grabbing and hugging Bobby. "Fucking Charlie can't take this guy out any time anywhere" Barnett said out loud for all to hear. "But what I really wanna know is how the hell did 'Charlie' miss shooting one of those two monster ears?"

"Fuck you Barnett" came the obligatory reply from Joyce who gave Barnett a big bear hug anyway. Everyone knew that Bobby was not bragging or patting himself on the shoulders what he stated to his buddies later on after meal time. During that battle he was wounded in, Joyce used every tool Uncle Sam gave him and trained him for, Bobby expressed that he has no regrets for ending the lives of a minimum 15 N.V.A. soldiers.

Joyce continued on with the event saying that during all of the madness, the yelling and screaming that was happening, one of the squad members whom he could not identify at that time was a killing machine. "When that bayonet went into my side I had a searing deep burning pain that practically immobilized me. That gook soldier was just about to stick me again when and all I can say is well, it's hard to describe. The eyes of that soldier suddenly became as large as the moon; it looked as if they were going to pop right out of his head! He just stopped, stopped right there from trying to kill me; a look of absolute fear was on his face even though I was the one being stabbed. He said something in Vietnamese; it sounded like 'su'chet', and then he dropped dead on the spot.

There was one of the guys who were very close to me but I couldn't make out which one of you who it was, he was just laying waste to them. Whoever it was, thanks a lot man I owe you my life." As always, standing away from the rest of the squad, off in the back end of the tent, Tod Moros silently nodded, acknowledging Bob Joyce.

In that battle, Tod Moros sent many N.V.A. to the afterlife.

Specialist fourth class in rank Roy Tschudy would be described as a nice kid. The youngest member of the squad at eighteen years of age he respected and revered his 'brother's.' Roy Boy as he was called by the others always wanted to be accepted as an equal among the team and did his best to fit in. Although most of the squad was only one or two years older than Tschudy, he believed they were all smarter and wiser then he was.

Roy Boy had grown up in an inner city with a single parent household, his father having died when Roy was five years old. Roy Boy still had a few nice memories of his dad; this gave him a small comfort to be able to remember and hold onto those thoughts. Roy had a sister Lennore who was one year younger than him and still living at home with their mom. One thing the Army or anyone else could never strip from him was the love and respect he held for his mother, as a widow she worked two jobs and never took a dime that wasn't earned.

Growing up was a little tough for Roy; without a dad to help guide him along and family finances poor he focused on the thing that was natural for him, athletics with a passion for sports. An average to below average student in school contrasted to his excellent athleticism. The members of the squad each loved him and respected Roy Boy equally as they did one another. This was an extended family inclusive of each one, one for all and all for one.

"One does not need to see the cloak of DEATH when in battle, in war; DEATH is always near and around."

CHAPTER 9

"Stop! Your killing me! Stop! "Bruce Mcclintock and Ray Ray were arguing between them which team would win the 1969 Super Bowl game. The New York Jets versus the Baltimore Colts, " Johnny Unitas is the best quarterback who ever played the game" Ray exclaimed. "He's washed up," Bruce retorted the best Q.B. is "Joe Willie Namath and the JETS, J-E-T-S, Jets are winning this thing I'm telling ya." Just like any two other guys who love football and sports in general, the difference being both are in a war zone half way around the world from their homes.

Mcclintock and Ray bantered back and forth which team was better and why they believed the team each one has rooted for since childhood would win. The big game was scheduled to be played on January 13th 1969 a Sunday afternoon; the 12 hour time zone difference meant the game would be played late that night in Vietnam.

SP5 Sgt. Dwight Studway was the designated Sergeant for perimeter guard duty of the base camp that night. The flight line that is aligned along the western part of the base with stored aircraft consisting of Chinook helicopters, Huey's, Cobra gunships and fixed wing planes. The airfield runway was made up of MARSTION MAT also known as

PSP which is perforated steel matting. Basically it is steel planking used for temporary runways and landing strips.

Approximately fifty yards further west from the area airstrip are twelve enforced sandbag security bunkers each was manned by soldiers either chosen or who were assigned on steady guard duty. Their weapons for the most part were their issued M-16 rifles with additional rounds inside ammo box's two per each bunker. These same bunkers were aligned the length of the flight line spread approximately twenty yards apart from one another. Each bunker was designed in a square shape image made up of sandbags three feet high and four feet in width although it varied in some aspects, containing two assigned soldiers of the guard per bunker. The "COMMAND BUNKER" was established in the center of all the other bunkers and devised somewhat different from the other bunkers. Since this was the main communication area between Headquarters and the others, it required special attention. The command bunker is larger in size than the other bunkers with the addition of a sandbag roof which was protection from rain and the elements. A communication radio system set up with phone lines stretching from Headquarters to the main bunker was in place for direct contact. During the monsoon season rain will fall in torrents soaking completely any that are exposed. Those who were in the two man bunkers used their ponchos attempting to stay somewhat dry, still a losing proposition.

Sergeant Studway made the assignments for the twelve bunkers and issued the standard orders that governed engagement fire. He then chose the five guardsmen who would be assigned with him inside the main bunker. Larger and with more men, it seemed almost cozy and relaxed inside for sure any assigned to it had was the envy of the other men. Another benefit to this particular bunker was having an M-60 machine gun mounted in the front center facing forward directly into the jungle.

Ah yes, the jungle. The base camp Commanding officer was either, stupid, negligent, or ill informed with regard to the demographics between the bunkers protecting the flight line along with the entire base camp and the close proximity to the jungle itself.

The men who performed steady guard duty on a nightly basis often stated their concerns, feeling that the overgrowth of jungle was close enough to the bunkers which gave them the feeling they could almost reach out and touch the grassy leafs protruding from it.

"Pssst Ray, c'mon over here by me, we can listen to the game together on my transistor radio," Bruce motioned to Ray Ray. Armed Forces Radio was airing the game; both Ray and Bruce sat back on their bunks preparing to listen to the game. Bensky ambled over along with Jaybird and Lee Pelton. Fink opened a bag of chips from his just received care package from home, the bag was half way open and Pelton already had a handful of WISE Potato chips out of the bag heading straight into his wide open mouth.

BOOM! Followed by four louder BOOMS, airfield warning siren squealing a high pitched decibel noise meant one thing only. Mcclintock threw his radio on his bed, both he and Ray along with the rest of the squad scrambled out of their tent weapons in hand, ammo bandoliers strung over the shoulder to meet the attack they knew was on.

The dark midnight sky was aglow with flares giving the entire area the look of daylight hour. Vietcong sappers had entered the base camp cutting through the perimeter concertina wire maneuvering undetected between the main command bunker and the smaller two manned bunkers. Once past those two bunkers, the sappers slyly continued past the flight line and placed their explosives on as many aircrafts as possible which were then blown up and destroyed in a synchronized manner.

Confusion ran amok; those stationed on perimeter guard duty found themselves totally surprised now turning 180 degrees and began firing at the enemy sappers who were now to the back of them. Warrant officers and other pilots ran quickly to assigned ships to get them airborne A.S.A.P., weapon fire coming in all directions without any type of battlefield positions established.

Members of the nut group squad arrived at the point of attack within two minutes from their tent area, some grouped up, and others did not have a chance to do so. Roy Boy found himself separated, alone in the midst of the surprise attack and quickly settled down into a small rut like opening in the ground still behind the airfield. Heart racing like a jacked up motor in a flashy car, adrenalin pumping faster than ever before, his M-16 at the ready and flipped on automatic, Roy Boy began to open fire.

Admittedly, Roy Boy never took aim at the enemy but instinctively was aware of their proximity, hell; he couldn't tell you if he even shot or killed an enemy sapper. With six magazines three in each side pants pocket, Roy Boy was certain that this was the night he would meet his fate. Startled suddenly, Roy observed a somewhat familiar figure stop behind him for a second looking down at him and then rush by him like the wind.

Tod Moros observed Roy Boy alone firing his weapon, in a flash Moros flew past him, Moros was in his element. Although Roy Boy was thin and wiry, he was by no means extra strong or even strong for that matter. Strength wise average would be the best description for him. Roy was amped up the adrenalin was sky high, if he did find himself in any sort of hand to hand combat he was sure that he would prevail. No conceit implied, no braggadocio, Roy Boy just knew it.

Glancing to the tree line, Roy Tschudy saw the dawn's daylight sun breaking through the jungle and onto the base camp. All the firing had stopped a while back but seemed like it still was happening at the present, strange. "Form up in a straight line" Lieutenant Peter Marino gave an order for all who were in ear shot, "straight line from the airfield straight out past the bunkers into the jungle perimeter" pointing his finger forward as he gave his directive. "Keep your spacing and weapons at the ready" he continued, any enemy movement considered hostile, waste em!" "If they are wounded try and take him as a prisoner, be smart, move out!"

Bobby Joyce, Jaybird Fink and Roy Boy linked up walking in a straight line as directed looking at the dead and there were plenty of them. In Roy's mind he couldn't help but think back to when he was a little kid watching a Disney movie named "Tonka", in it was a scene from the Little Big Horn or Custer's Last Stand. After that battle, the enemy dead was strewn across the battlefield, bodies everywhere. Crazy as it may seem but that was the impression 18 year old SP/4 Roy Tschudy was thinking.

"Look at this shit" Joyce stated pointing at two dead

sappers. Laying five feet in front and to our right was one body fully intact with his head split wide open, the sun rising had shards of sunrays displaying the cavity of the dead soldiers cranium. "Looks like someone polished the inside of his head" Jaybird said to both Joyce and Roy Boy. "Where the fuck is his brains?" Fink asked, "Look down at your boots pal" Roy Boy said. Fully perfect as a neurosurgeon had removed it, the sapper's brain lay on the ground. Roy picked up a midsized rock walked over to it and dropped the rock into the brain which actually swallowed it up making a sound like 'THUCK.' In unison all three members of the squad looking down at the obliterated brain matter and said exactly at that moment, FUCK YOU, and moved on with the line.

One very noticeable trait on at least four of the dead sappers was each pinkie finger nail was extra long in the shape of a Jai Alai racket. The assumption being that these now dead combatants would use the nail to scoop and snort cocaine or some sort of drug; in essence they were going on a suicide mission and needed a little extra bravery.

Jay Fink along with Tschudy observed the last body bag being removed from the command bunker. The two of them entered into the large bunker only to witness a scene of utter destruction. That certain smell an odor which can only be identified with DEATH was detected immediately. Blood covering the entire bunker floor so thick and coagulated, the boots of both Jay and Roy made sucking sounds as they walked about inside the large bunker surveying the scene. In the middle center wooden post a small piece of human skull was half way imbedded along with a shard of sharp shrapnel containing dark strands of hair attached to it.

Jaybird reached out and in both a tender and respectful manner pulled the shrapnel free from the center post; nothing was spoken between the two soldiers. Fink holding the piece of metal and skull in his hands with Tschudy exited the Command bunker walking five to ten feet away. Both soldiers dropped to a knee as Roy dug out a small hole in the ground with his bare hands. Jay gingerly placed the remains into the freshly dug hole; both men covered it reverently. Still no words exchanged between them, only a silent nod and they both moved on, back to patrol.

Sergeant Dwight Studway along with five other soldiers assigned to that Command Bunker perished in the nights attack, those souls never had a chance. 'Charlie' had long planned this attack mainly for disruption and damage to aircrafts, they also were well aware of how near the jungle it was to the perimeter guard bunkers. The enemy coordinated attack of blowing up the main bunker with a sapper charge at the same time explosives went off, destroyed two Chinooks, three Huey's and one fixed wing aircraft. This not only disabled all communications between Head Quarters, and the command bunker, it created chaos between the Americans and accomplished 'Charlie's' mission.

As usual or as always being the case, Tod Moros stood back inside the squad tent replaying the kills made the others were unaware of. Feeling a cold chill run down his back, Roy Boy turned his head and just stared at the back end of the tent in the direction where Tod was standing. Being cold as ice without any emotion, the killer Tod Moros simply returned Roy's stare without a word spoken. I wouldn't know how to describe that interaction between them, they both silently knew.

63

Thirty six hours after the base camp attack, members of the 18th Engineer Brigade created a fifty yard wide open area from the perimeter bunker system to the Jungle. Many soldiers muttered among themselves this was another example of some asshole with bars on his shoulders who was clueless, a little late for the guys who made the ultimate sacrifice don't you think?

"Hey Mash, where did you do your basic training at? John Palmero asked John Mash while both were taking a dump at the same time in the base camp latrine. With his olive drab jungle fatigues dangling down at his ankles, Mash plainly replied, Fort Jackson South Carolina and then I was shipped out to Fort Polk Lose-e-anna for A.I.T. (Advanced Infantry Training) how about you?" Twirling three square sheets of the remaining toilet paper in his right hand Palmero replied, "flew me all the way to Fort Ord California and then I stayed there for my A.I.T." "You lucky prick, California you got hot looking women and I got snakes, bugs, and crotch rot, sound fair to you?" Palmero laughed and said "more than fair to me!"

The fact of the matter is Fort Polk as many have claimed, is geographically WORSE than the Nam. Bruce Mcclintock also had his A.I.T. there and said to me that Nam was like Hawaii compared to POLK! "What a shit hole, swamps, snakes, gators and fucking bugs that look like they come from another world" Mash went on. "Hey, how much paper is left on that roll your holding?" "Enough to wipe "MY" ass pal, good thing you had that tough training down there in Fort Polk" as Palmero scrunched the three tiny sheets into one and proceeded to stick it in the crevice of his behind. Once again the obligatory reply as standard operating procedure from Mash was, "FUCK YOU."

Cleaning their weapons, preparing items needed for patrol, Brian Barnett chimed in upon hearing what Palmero told the squad about regarding his shit house conversation with Mash. "When I got off the bus at the so called welcoming center in Fort Jackson, we were met by this tough looking Sergeant who began screaming at all of us at the top of his lungs" Barnett in his sorry southern accent went on. "Hew sonsabitches Yankee booha, yaba daba muddershits." We were all northern guys and looked at each other like what the hell did he say? The next thing I know is all of us are nose in the dirt doing pushups and told to eat shit!" Fucking rebels were still fighting the Civil War; no one must have told them that in between now and then were WW1, WW2, Korea, and now Vietnam.

Larry Bensky began "I came over to Nam on a boat, a freaking troop carrier named the U.S.S. UPSHUR. I'll never forget the name of that boat; it took T-H-I-R-T-Y F-U-C-K-I-N-G D-A-Y-S" said Larry, dragging out the words to emphasize exactly just how long thirty days are in total. The company I originally was assigned to the 271st Aviation Company, 10th Aviation Group 1st Aviation Brigade left Long Beach California late January 1st and we arrived in Nam on the 31st, THE BEGINNING OF THE TET OFFENSIVE! For shits sake how's that for a welcoming?"

We were all puking our guts out on that crappy little boat, some guys had the dry heaves complaining their ribs felt like they were being crushed, screw the Navy and the oceans they ride on." Lee Pelton stood up and answered Bensky, "I flew over on a nice Jet plane with pretty stewardesses and even got ice cream. Also by the way Bensky, it's called a ship not a boat" Larry gave Pelton the look of, "ARE YOU SHITTIN ME? Larry immediately began thinking what he would like to do to Pelton and his ice-cream cone.

CHAPTER 10

The flap of the squad tent flew open, Roger DuPont declared to the men, "I need two volunteers, Roy Boy and Pelton your it!" "What the "F" is that about?" Lee Pelton shot back. "Our squads turn for two guys on shit burning detail" explained Roger the dodger. Roy Boy in disgust asked Roger DuPont why the two of them were 'volunteered?' "Because everyone else has already done it before except the two of you, now it's you're up at bat boys."

Pelton and Roy would rather have been ordered on a two man secret mission to Hanoi trying to capture Ho Chi Minh than be on the shit burning detail. With a look of resignation on their face both squad members rose and began moving out for the detail. "Good luck, have fun, don't eat any of it," the rest of the guys laughingly yelled out from behind them. Pelton and Tschudy gave the obligatory "FUCK YOU" in return, which made the rest of the squad laugh even louder.

The only way to describe SHIT BURNING DETAIL is that it is one big shitty detail. Pelton and Roy Boy signed out a truck and headed over to the first of the three base camp latrines constructed in the manner of a small wooden outhouse. Inside, carved out of a long piece of sheet wood are four medium sized holes side by side for the soldiers to sit and empty their bowels. The outside of the latrine has four trap doors with each door owning the lower one third of a 55 gallon metal drum, each drum containing either gasoline or fuel diesel for the shit to burn.

Opening the trap door felt like someone punched you in the face! Stink of all stinks, the mother lode of smell so noxious like a hand reaching down your mouth and back up your nose filled with the odor of shit. Ugghh! "Hey Lee, be careful loading these suckers onto the truck, remember what happened to D'agostino the time he had this detail." God save me from that thought" Lee replied back. Previously one of the platoon members named D'agostino and his partner who was assigned to the Shit burning detail hurried to get the job done, in their haste doing so they lifted the heavy drum out from the small cubby hole it was in too fast and dropped it onto the rear end of the truck so hard it sounded with a loud thud.

Like an incoming enemy mortar round, a huge brown 'TURD' came flying out of the drum landing squarely on the top of D'agostinos head! Poor D'agostino began running in circles and screaming at the top of his lungs for a medic. He ran full speed towards the first aid station with a large piece of shit on his head and gasoline piss running down the front of his face, I think he would rather have been shot. "I know I'd rather be shot than having someone's freakin TURD on my head" said Roy Boy, "No doubt" answered Lee Pelton as the two of them diligently went about completion of their assigned 'DUTY.'

"UNCLE SAM" is ingenious for the way it can mold young men into the machine it wants and needs. It does not matter if the soldier is an inductee or he chose to enlist, "your heart may belong to mama, but your ass belongs to UNCLE SAM." Given to each brand new soldier is his new identity, RA11909799 sample for the enlisted man, US55709668 for the draftee. Name patch adorned above the left breast pocket solely for the rebel Drill Instructor to mispronounce the name of the new G.I., and are reminded of that specific fact on a daily basis, all of us are now "GOVERNMENT ISSUE" A.K.A. G.I.'s. Let's not forget the spiffy new crew cuts provided free of charge, tips are appreciated now get the hell out.

Assembled in the basic training course that lasts for eight weeks does not include the first three days for 'Orientation' plus a "Zero week" prior to the beginning of the course. The beginning of stripping away '<u>YOU</u>' for the purpose of making '<u>US</u>' has now begun in full force.

Another thing during this time, the D.I.'s could give a fart squeak less on what you have previously accomplished, what or who you know, what your education level is, portfolios or anything closely resembling what was BEFORE ENTERING THE U.S. ARMY! What the drill instructors DID care about was making the new recruit fit to run, jump, crawl, shoot, fight, and learn the art of KILL.

The bottom line is it's all about teamwork, learning to work as a unit relying on the skill sets that has been drummed into each soldier. After being deemed proficient on all levels of the above, the now molded graduated soldiers are given a job title or as directed an M.O.S. (Military Occupational Code). This code will identify a specific job which each soldier will be assigned. It should be noted that not every soldier ends up working the M.O.S. assigned; different situations can dictate a change of venue.

Without a nice summer vacation the new soldier is now sent directly from "Boot Camp" to their designated area of assignment for an additional eight weeks of training in A.I.T. (Advanced Infantry Training) on the specific tactics to be used in that M.O.S. Many young men are then sent to the Far East on the other side of the world, to a place named Vietnam. Either as a replacement for a soldier who has rotated back home after the standard one year tour of duty, or for a soldier who has been wounded in action, or to replace another who was killed in action.

Between four to five months prior to arriving in a war zone, before entering the service, this soldier that was raised by parents and who taught him the golden rule, to value life, have ethics, and principals is now different, much more so. If fortunate enough to return back to the world without physical injury, the young soldier nevertheless will be changed forever.

Then there are some who like to kill, even relish it. The power of holding life or death at his command makes the feeling for him of being invincible. Killers, born or created? Tod Moros knew it was his responsibility, his job is to kill. If asked that thought about being born as one who was a killer or if for whatever reason created to become a serial killer, the response would probably be…not answered.

Tod never explained the aspect of DEATH to the squad never shared his opinion on DEATH or the taking of lives many times over, like everything else about him, he kept it to himself. Tod Moros was distinctly different in thought and deed from all others in the squad, platoon, company, and even the whole damn brigade!

"The cold hand of DEATH steals the last breath of life or is it a warm embrace from DEATH that releases the fear of it?"

Tod Moros accepts both concepts delivering DEATH in many ways. Tod is a killer, a taker of lives, it really does not matter which way it ends, just so it does. Tod is strict and regimented always adheres to the kill plan chosen. Secretly and unbeknownst to the squad, Tod Moros will only take orders, special orders, from the Commanding Officer. This is the main reason Tod will not engage those in the named NUT SQUAD with anything personal.

Tod Moros is a PROFESSIONAL KILLER, unequalled in the ability to take a life. The Commanding Officer has designated specifics for Moros, certain tasks other soldiers can do and who also perform, BUT NOT to the degree that Moros can. The C.O. has Moros portfolio before him knowing the long history of this elite DEATH MACHINE, always obeying the orders and does as commanded. Moros is a good soldier, keeps quiet, keeps his distance, and follows orders… to perfection!

Bruce Mcclintock slowed to a halt simultaneously raising his right arm with fist clenched just above his shoulder indicating to squad leader Roger DuPont to halt, DuPont immediately did the same for the squad. Like a fine tuned engine that runs as smooth as possible, the squad members took up a defensive position. Ten or twelve yards off to his right on the jungle path Mcclintock caught a glimpse of some sort of quick movement out of the corner of his eye.

The movement was subtle, so slight that only the

trained eye of a professional would take note. This being one of the main reasons why all members of the squad opted to have Bruce Mcclintock walk point and the same for Mcclintock as well. Inching forward towards the area of concern with a "God given antenna" raised high, a hidden enemy tunnel was now detected. Finding the location of a tunnel is difficult enough, finding the size and what is in that tunnel is even more of a challenge.

Roger DuPont eyed the small opening then he signaled over to the platoon Sergeant, a grizzly older veteran who was only addressed as 'Ryle.' Four days earlier, one of the two Tunnel Rats in the platoon Tony Lombardi was severely wounded by a Vietcong sniper and sent out to a hospital in Da Nang. Fortunately, Will Winter was available for the job.

Ryle ordered a small perimeter to be set up with squad members surveying a designated quadroon. With extra caution for external booby traps left behind by the enemy the squad scanned looking for a secondary tunnel entrance. Winter stripped off his olive drab jungle fatigue shirt and began to cover the upper extremities of his body with dirt.

William Winter was a student of the enemy and its culture, he interrogated captured enemy soldiers both men and women, ate the same food as them, bathed in rivers like they did, smelled as they do, essentially William Winter was one and the same as the enemy, the only difference being he was on our side!

There are many very good and heroic soldiers performing the job of a Tunnel Rat but let's be clear on this, there may be some as good as Will Winter, but it is near impossible to believe any are better!

Kneeling down at the mouth opening of the tunnel

Winter closes his eyes and seems to meditate for thirty seconds or so, removing his own made sharp honed blade from the sheath on his belt, Winter slides slowly head first into the abyss of the enemy lair, complete dark, complete silence.

All any of the rest of the men can do is wait, there is not a scintilla of contact between Winter and the squad, nothing. Inside William's mind, "inch along slow, slow, the wall is still rocky no signs yet. Uh huh, here it is, directions to my right for three feet, drop down." (The enemy devised a communication system inside the tunnels with carved indents into the wall. Where to turn, where a booby trap has been set, such as two step vipers which were snakes whose venom was so lethal one bite, two steps and your dead)

Armed with only his knife, sense of hearing and finger touch William Winter continued moving slowly in the direction map on the wall relying on his basic instincts. Winter although blind in the darkness of the tunnel, instinctively knows from many prior trips down a hell hole that something is within two feet of the corner. In a flash the pointed tip of Williams knife reaches around the mud wall corner and enters directly into the chest cavity of a waiting V.C The startled 'Charlie' only could expel the air from his lungs in response.

Winter shoved the dead soldier away being careful to do so, for the first time down any of the many previous tunnels, William actually thought he saw the outline of a figure that made him freeze in his spot. "Who, how, what?" All three questions presented at once, and then just like that, nothing. Winter took one long slow deep breath and slowly exhaled,

"Shit" he thought to himself "I need to take my R&R and I need to take it soon."

Three feet to the left of where the dead enemy soldier lay was a small portal that led to a further underground tunnel area. William removed the grass covering to the portal lying flat on his stomach quiet and listening, staying motionless for a long time, just kept listening. This was a tunnel system of immense proportions of which could possibly contain weapons, operating rooms, sleeping quarters, most probably other booby traps. William Winter decided it was wiser to report back with the information in hand rather than take any further chances continuing down into the dark abyss.

William Winter realizes he has been down in this tunnel for a long time without communication with the top, the platoon and squad do not have any idea on his status or if even Will Winter is still alive. The trip back to the surface is just as arduous as the one going down and maybe even more so. The tunnels are narrow and small; William must maneuver out of the tunnel in a BACKWARDS motion. Relying on his memory and touch, Will Winter is pulled by the boots out from his hell on earth.

Sucking the canteen of water handed to him completely dry, number one Tunnel Rat Will Winter submits a full oral report on his survey findings to Captain Riddell. Riddell hugs and then salutes young Winter, "You are one great tough fucking Tunnel Rat Winter; I will make sure you receive the proper recognition for this job! Hot Damn, get the blow torches out men, let's blow this sucker up!"

Sitting alone and replaying his time in the tunnel, William Winter could not shake the feeling he was being observed in the darkness of the tunnel. William knew it would not be possible for anyone at all to be in that small area at the same time, a physical impossibility, still Will Winter could not shake the thought.

Tod Moros actually ALMOST cracked a smile as Winter sat there pondering the past few hours. Tod knew how William felt, after all when it came to dealing with killing and taking a life there was none better than Moros doing the deadly deed.

"Death is stealthy, moving silent and secret, Death watches near and far."

CHAPTER 11

Half sitting, half lying on his cot with his left leg bent so he could rest his chin on it, Ray was quiet and contemplating. "Hey, whatsamatter you?" Bruce Mcclintock asked trying a bit of levity. Ray Ray tilted his head slightly, through pursed lips he replied to Mcclintock "when was the last time you received a letter from home or from anyone else for that matter?" "Geez, Haven't given it much thought pal, you are aware the squad has been busy." "Yeah, yeah, I know but something ain't right here Bruce, I can't put my finger on it but something ain't right, I can just feel it."

Now that Ray brought the subject up Bruce tried to remember when was the last he received his own mail, "I'll be damned if I can remember the last time we had mail call, gotta be some kind of Army screw up." Bobby Joyce overheard the conversation between the two squad members and reminded them that since orders came down from H.Q. two days ago stating the entire platoon and Company is now preparing to rotate back to the states the company most likely issued a hold put on mail deliveries.

Both DuPont and Jon Mash concurred with Joyce, "I agree, they're holding the mail until we get back stateside" said John Palmero, "they don't want it crisscrossing all over the place." The conversation slowly ended, each squad member now beginning the happy task of stowing their gear, packing all necessary items for the return back to the world. No more snakes, no more bugs, no more mosquitoes and monsoons, no more C-rations and cold showers, no more patrol and no more 'CHARLIE.' No more war and no more fighting, no more, no more. Going home, FINALLY.

Laying in their cots later in the evening prior to leaving on the "Big Bird" that will fly the entire Company home, the squad heard a quiet conversation just outside of their tent taking place. Captain Glenn Riddell was speaking in a low hushed voice that was barely audible, this was odd due to the fact Riddell never spoke in a soft manner at any time. The words were clear, they were concise, but the words did not make any sense to any of the squad, all of whom were straining to hear from the dark quiet of their tent.

"I am saddened, it makes me sick to my stomach," Captain Riddell stated. "Fine young men all, such a total waste of life. They will always be the best damn squad under my command, any command, I just finally finished the last condolence letter to a family." Roy Boy sat up with a quizzical look on his face, whispering, to the others "does anyone know what the Cap is talking about, who he's talking about?" Not one squad member could begin to comprehend who or what Captain Riddell was alluding to, in an odd way all of them were in a dream like sense. John Palmero with the thought of his beloved Susan pictured in his mind wondered aloud, "I don't understand, is the Captain talking about us, does this mean we're not going back home?"

"You are going home, 'except'... (Pause) it's not the home any of you were thinking." An unfamiliar voice began to speak and address the men of this squad at the same time slowly emerging out from the dark rear corner of the tent. Upon hearing that unfamiliar voice an unearthly silence fell over them, each of their minds in a whirl as if exiting off a high speed rollercoaster.

At long last, Tod Moros now stood before this squad of soldiers, all eyes fixed on him. With a deep voice that was neither loud nor threatening the tall lean dark shadowy figure of Tod Moros stood standing front and center in the middle of their tent. Tod Moros continued on, "All of you have seen me before and many times over. YOU KNOW WHO I AM; YOU KNOW (again with a slight Pause) WHAT I AM." Shocked, in disbelief, no one moved to interrupt Tod Moros not even William Winter who was visiting Roger DuPont inside their squad tent.

"All of you have seen me on the battle fields; you have seen me take lives in battle while I have always watched over you just as you 'thought' to have seen me. I have been with each of you many different times and yet also at the same time, I have been here ever since the dawn of time. YOU KNOW WHO I AM, I AM SINGULAR yet I AM MANY, I AM TOD MOROS, I DRIVE MORTALS TO THEIR DEADLY FATE, I AM DEATH, I AM …ENDLESS.

Life is not yours it never belonged to you; it is a gift not to be measured in years only valued by what you have done in those years."

Every single squad member sat in silence, in shock, in fear. Each soldier began reflecting on his own memories, replaying a certain incident that happened to them over the past weeks or was it months? Roy now understood who was standing for an instant behind him on January 13th, Bobby

Joyce sat there on his cot remembering the bayonet wound deep into his side and the medic pleading with Joyce to "stay with me" as the light slowly dimmed from his eyes.

Both Jon Mash and Ray Ray both recalled the night they were heading back to their tent after the extra chow time when Jon Mash swore that he could see someone or some figure out beyond the perimeter line and later that night with Ray having terrible dreams. Instantly both knew who was there and now he was standing in the midst of them.

Bruce Mcclintock also remembered back to that day on patrol when he caught some movement out of the corner of his eye then signaling the squad to stop. That figure was Tod Moros; a sudden chill ran down Mcclintocks back.

William Winter realizing what he thought he had seen in that deep dark tunnel earlier was true. One by one, it became clear to each squad member, each and everyone, an incident of their own personal war time experience was in fact their final one.

Tod Moros was collectively aware of each soul in the tent, Tod Moros inherently knew their questions and fears along with the realization of who he is and wondering what will happen next to each of them.

"I have walked battle fields from the beginning of time, since mankind has decided to engage with wars; I have watched and looked, I am the taker of life. It is who I am, it is what I do. I answer to only the Supreme Being the omnipotent one, the Commander Officer if you will, of all.

TOD MOROS in all of his existence, never, not one time felt compassion or pity unto his charges, DEATH is devoid of feelings and emotions. Millions of battles with countless souls have crossed the path of the entity MOROS without the smallest of feelings. TOD MOROS for the first and may be the only time through the rest of eternity came to know the depth of love shared between this squad, this very special squad.

"Fear not for your souls you young men of honor, I have watched, you have acquitted yourself with grace and honor on the battle fields of war. As you walked the path in war I have always followed from behind, watching. I follow no more; my job with each of you is now complete, rest easy young souls, go now and receive your just reward, you are going "HOME."

"FALL IN!" Came the last order, Mcclintock, take the point. The rest of the squad assumed their regular line positions then started their final patrol, towards the light which God the SUPREME COMMANDER WAS SHOWING THEM, POINTING THE WAY BACK HOME.

CHAPTER 12

*Standing shoulder to shoulder heaviness close to their breast, Lucius and Gaius both knew their return to Rome and the humiliation of defeat for Rome could only end in one way. As their own thoughts became shared as one, a cold hand from behind pressed down upon the shoulder on each of them. Both Roman Commanders turned their heads peering into the eyes of a familiar figure.

"Greetings, allow me to introduce myself." With a deep voice that was neither loud nor threatening the Roman soldier continued, I am ANGELUS MORTIS, both of you have seen me before and many times over. YOU KNOW WHO I AM, YOU KNOW (a slight Pause) WHAT I AM. Shocked, in disbelief, neither Lucius nor Gaius moved to interrupt Angelus Mortis. "You have seen me on the battle fields, I have been with each of you many different times and yet also at the same time, I have been here since the dawn of time. YOU KNOW WHO I AM, each one of you do. I have watched you from afar and up close, you have seen me take lives in battle while always watching you as you 'thought' to have seen me. Life is not yours it never belonged to you, it is a gift not to be measured in years but valued by what you have done in those years."

"I have walked battle fields from the beginning of time, since mankind has decided to engage with wars; I have watched and looked, I am the taker of life. It is who I am, it is what I do.

"I am neither Roman nor Greek not Jew or Pagan, I am singular yet many. I am ANGELUS MORTIS; I AM THE ANGEL OF DEATH, I AM AND WILL ALWAYS WILL BE...ENDLESS!"

THE END.

TOD MOROS or ANGELUS MORTUS, whichever name has been prescribed for the description of this being, entity, named DEATH, remains a mystery to all mortal beings. Many people fear the mere mention of the word especially the connotation related with it. Dark and foreboding, sadness coupled with grief leaves the feeling of a large hole in the heart for family and friends of loved soldiers who have passed over.

TOD MOROS is the entity who stalks the battle fields that mortals have created since the beginning of days. For every battle or skirmish, firefight or anything else where man bears ill will for another, TOD MOROS IS PRESENT.

MOROS or ANGELUS the same entity.

We cannot comprehend the entirety of MOROS, cannot understand the how or why the full measurement of WAR DEATH. TOD MOROS is a spirit, an entity whose existence was granted in the beginning of days. Because man has decided that the gift of life entrusted from the Supreme Being, our God Creator, is not shared with dignity and mutual respect, TOD MOROS begins the task to which assigned. DEATH is abundant all over the Earth, every second of every minute of every day and week, everywhere and anywhere. The taking of life, this is the job of DEATH. MOROS is the entity who is DEATH who is only found in fields of battle, it is an entity of one yet many, in one place yet also in others as well. Why my son? Why my husband or why my brother? Moros takes, God receives.

MOROS does not have any boundaries, nor do rules and regulations apply for the objective of the aims. It is what it is, DEATH answers to no one, MOROS takes life on the fields of battle when or where it decides. The souls of soldier combatants whether one side or the other are selected by TOD MOROS and only TOD MOROS. DEATH has been bestowed the insight of knowing from the beginning, seeing into the hearts and souls of combat soldiers.

Battle lines that have been drawn between nations, religions, and race are of no matter to MOROS, it is of no importance to whom is selected, who has been chosen. Many good souls have breathed a last earthly breath from both sides of the field of fire, the ego of us mortals always assumes we are the righteous ones and the other is the evil, pis'sha!

The soldiers selected for eternity are not judged by this spirit, this is not now or ever was any part of the directed path given, and the taker of lives does not discriminate. The kingdom is abundant with soldier's souls even if they did take lives in battle against each another. War is never created by those selected to do the battle rather it is created by those who prefer to send others, usually the young. Those who braved the risk of DEATH are not judged by it, their hearts filled with honor along with bravery and compassion.

The end of the last breath is the beginning of a new life with "the One."

TOD MOROS is the one who makes the decision on the swiftness or not for the end of a life, MOROS plans each move methodically for the soldier now chosen to leave his physical body. Knowing each soul and whether goodness is in that soldier or the decisions to be corrupt within that soul, leads TOD MOROS to either place a cold hand upon that soldier's shoulder or to embrace him with the warmth of God's peace. Each and every soldier who has been in harm's way has indeed seen TOD MOROS and or ANGELUS MORTUS; one way or another they all have seen MOROS and have been seen in return.

DEATH, THY NAME IS

Death has many, many names attributed from different cultures, beliefs and mythology. Death is perceived in male form, while in others,

AZTEC MYTHOLOGY: 'MITECACIHUATI,' A female known as the CHIEF DEATH GODDESS.

SLAVIC MYTHOLOGY: The name for DEATH is 'MORANA.'

POLAND: 'SMIREC' DEATH, female skeletal woman.

ROMAN MYTH NAME: 'LIBITINA' Goddess of the corpses, funerals, and the dead.

HINDU: 'YAMA' God of DEATH.

CANAANITES: 'MOT' Personified as a god of DEATH.

CELTIC MYTHOLOGY: 'BRETON' Spectral figure portending DEATH.

NORSE MYTHOLOGY: Personified in the shape of 'HEL,' the goddess of DEATH.

MEXICO: 'SANTA MUERTA' Our lady of the HOLY DEATH.

DEATH: 'GRIM REAPER.'

VIETNAMESE: 'SU' CHE'T,' DEATH.

LATIN: 'ANGELUS MORTIS,' ANGEL OF DEATH.

DC UNIVERSE: 'THE ENDLESS' meaning DEATH.

GERMAN: 'TOD' meaning DEATH...Pronounced as 'TOTE.'

GREEK: 'MOROS' In Greek mythology, MOROS is the being of impending doom, which drives mortals to their deadly fate.

*Now you the reader have properly been introduced to one of the main characters in this book, HE WHO IS THE <u>ENDLESS</u>, Also known as <u>TOD</u> <u>MOROS</u> also for the Roman soldiers, <u>ANGELUS</u> <u>MORTIS</u>.

TOD MOROS

CHAPTER 13

LETTERS LEFT AT THE WALL
TEDDY BEAR

People leave things at THE Wall: medals, old jungle boots, books of poetry, notes, toys, a teddy bear. ..a tattered teddy bear. I pictured a boy's mother reaching into a closet where things had gone untouched for years. I saw her open a box. Perhaps she didn't want to remember what was in that box, but she opened it. She saw the teddy bear and fell upon it, holding it tightly as she held her son.

The bear was her baby's companion. He toddled around with it, hugged it, held it by it's arm, and carried it to bed. It kept away the monsters of the night. Everyday he would tell her what he and the bear had done. And when she rocked him to sleep, holding this bear, he fought sleep, eyes closing slowly, as he would later fight death.

The bear waited a long time in that box with nothing to do-no one to protect. The mother found it and took it to her son. Not to a cemetery of strangers, but to THE WALL, the still peaceful place where her son is among friends. There again with his boy, the bear can rest. The monsters are gone.

And more than anyone else, more even than the mother, the boy and his 58,000 friends understand.

I could cry my heart out.

You fought in a war and died and part of me died with you.

I'm still fighting a war I know I can never win, trying to live without you. My heart is broken forever.

No one knows how hard it is to love and lose, until they have gone through it. I carry you in my mind every minute of my life.

I talk to your picture and say I love you and miss you and want to so very, very bad, but honey, pictures can't talk back.

If love and tears could have saved you, you would be here today.

I'm sitting here talking to you tonight the way we used to do, but I can't hold your hand and say Mom loves you.

When you came back, they wouldn't even let me touch you. I didn't think that was fair. You are my son and I will never forgive them. I gave birth to you and raised you and I begged so hard just to put my arms around you and kiss you goodbye.

I will never forget you. Your memories are my treasures. I will never let them go.

As I look around at the thousands of other names, I remember that each name here represents, on average, 20 years that each boy was some Momma's little boy as you were mine. I miss you so Jimmy.

<u>BILLY</u>

I am the one who rocked him as a baby.
I'm the one who kissed away the hurts.
I'm the one who taught him right from wrong.
I'm the one who held him for the last time
and watched him fly away to war.
I'm the one who prayed each night
"Dear God keep him safe."
I'm the goofy Mom who sent him a
Christmas tree in Vietnam.
I'm the one whose heart they broke when they
told me my Billy died in a helicopter crash.
And now I'm still the one who still cries at night
because of all the memories I have that will never die.
But you were so full of life and you kept me busy
for 21 years I had you, that now I thank God for
letting me be your Mom and for leaving me so
many more good memories than bad ones.
I LOVE YOU BILLY, AND I MISS YOU SO.

If I could just have the return of one day, I wonder which day I would pick?

Would it be the one where they said, "It's a Boy!" or the day that you took your first step?

Or the day you played a little league game, or the day you rode your bike alone for the first time? Or would it be the day you laughed as you happily said "Got my license Mom, now can I drive?"

Now I'll not hear you open the door and call out, Mom, I'm home, so what time do we eat?"

CHAPTER 14

BUT, LET'S SUPPOSE WHAT IF?

What if? TOD MOROS decided in his infinite wisdom OR DIRECTION not to place his cold hand upon each squad member's shoulder, what if TOD MOROS decided not to offer a warm embrace of finality?

Suppose instead the squad went on to live a full life, a life filled with the hopes and dreams all young men strive for. Suppose TOD MOROS devoid of emotions, without love or hate, without kindness or envy, suppose if you will TOD MOROS for just a second, observed this squad of soldiers and decided to let them find another destiny, LIFE!

ROGER DuPont, after leaving the military upon completion of his service, returned to the small home town where he was born and raised. Roger married his girlfriend, then one year later unmarried his girlfriend and remarried again. Roger did take up the generous offer of his Uncle to work with him along with becoming an apprentice plumber before actually owning the business. Roger now happily married and a dad retired from the job he came to love and became involved with the local Vietnam veterans chapter in his community volunteering his time in many of his chapter's events.

ROGER DUPONT is indeed a special man, a good man who has and continues to "give back" especially, regarding all other veterans. TOD MOROS is only a memory, still though, a real one.

LEE PELTON, after leaving the military upon completion of his service, also returned to the boyhood home where he was born and raised. Lee took a test for the local utilities company and ended up spending over thirty five years in their employment. LEE married his girlfriend and is still together after forty five years, Lee and his wife are parents to a couple of grown children who reside nearby.

Lee became an enthusiastic lover of vintage automobiles, he owns one or two and joined as a member of the HOT-RODDER'S CAR CLUB displaying his vehicles in classic old car shows. Lee now long retired from his career path became involved with his local Vietnam veterans chapter in his community volunteering his time in many of his chapter's events.

LEE PELTON is indeed a special man, a good man, who has and continues to "give back" especially, regarding all other veterans. In the same vein TOD MOROS is only a memory, still though, a real one.

JOHN PALMERO, after leaving the military upon completion of his service, also returned to the boyhood home where he was born and raised. John Palmero took advantage of the G.I. education bill and completed a four year degree as a book keeper for a large firm; John became a terrific cruncher of numbers. John Palmero married his sweet girlfriend Susan and they raised two beautiful girls now both married themselves and with kids of their own. John now long retired from his career path is a full time Grandpa and loving every minute of it became involved with his local Vietnam veterans chapter volunteering his time in many of his chapter's events.

JOHN PALMERO is indeed a special man, a good man, who has and continues to "give back" especially, regarding all other veterans. TOD MOROS is only a memory, still though, a real one.

JON MASH, after leaving the military upon his completion of service also returned to his boyhood home where he was born and raised. True to his thoughts, Mash took the test and worked for the N.Y.C. Sanitation Department for 35 years. Jon rose through the ranks of that department to become a Superintendent leading members in varying successful ways.

Mash met his dream girl near his home town and they have been married near fifty years. Their children a son and daughter became professionals in their own right, their son a medical doctor saves lives similar to his dad many years back. JON MASH became involved with his local Vietnam veteran's chapter in his community volunteering his time in many of his chapter's events.

JON MASH is indeed a special man, a good man, who has and continues to "give back" especially, regarding all other veterans. TOD MOROS is only a memory, still though, a real one.

JAY FINK, after leaving the military upon his completion of service also returned to the boyhood home where he was born and raised. Jaybird met the love of his life a lass named Heidi; they married and raised a son and daughter becoming Grandparents twice over.

JAY FINK became a Fireman with the NEW YORK CITY FIRE DEPARTMENT spending thirty two years before retiring on a disability. Jay was just as valiant working as a smoke eater much the same as was his service time in Nam saving many lives during his career. JAY "BIRD" FINK became involved with his local Vietnam veteran's chapter in his community volunteering his time in many of his chapter's events.

JAY is indeed a special man, a good man, who has and continues to "give back" especially, regarding all other veterans. TOD MOROS is only a memory, still though, a real one.

RAY RAY, after leaving the military upon his completion of service, returned to his boyhood home where he was born and raised. Ray entered into a successful business career and after over forty years is in a semi-retirement state, still working not for the money but to keep him busy.

RAY RAY married with a lovely wife having spent many anniversaries together also have grown adult children. Ray is devout in his faith to God, a good Catholic boy who is intent on helping others and most especially veterans. RAY RAY may be big in stature but is soft spoken and kind, RAY became involved with his local Vietnam veteran's chapter in his community along with a few other veteran groups volunteering his time in many of his chapter's events.

RAY RAY is indeed a special man, a good man, who has and continues to "give back" especially, regarding all other veterans. TOD MOROS is only a memory, still though, a real one.

BRIAN BARNETT, after leaving the military upon completion of his service, Brian returned to the boyhood home where he was born and raised. Brian became a business entrepreneur owning private enterprise in the haberdashery business along with becoming a proprietor in the food industry employing many people with jobs and incomes. Barnett married his girlfriend Rona raising their son a highly successful business man and daughter a Veterinarian who provides love and caring for God's little creatures.

BRIAN BARNETT became involved with his local Vietnam veteran's chapter in his community volunteering his time in many of his chapter's events.

BRIAN is indeed a special man, a good man, who has and continues to "give back" especially, regarding all other veterans. TOD MOROS is only a memory, still though, a real one.

BRUCE MCCLINTOCK, after leaving the military upon completion of his service, Bruce returned to the boyhood home where he was born and raised. Bruce married his Italian sweetheart Jackie and they raised two beautiful daughters between them. BRUCE MCCLINTOCK enjoyed a long and successful career with the United States Post Office eventually becoming a Post Office district manager earning the admiration from all who worked for and with him. As a boss, whenever he would hire a person to work for the Postal Office, Bruce would fly the flag half mast!

BRUCE MCCLINTOCK became involved with his local Vietnam veteran's chapter in his community volunteering his time in many of his chapter's events.

BRUCE is indeed a special man, a good man, who has and continues to "give back" especially, regarding all other veterans. TOD MOROS is only a memory, still though, a real one.

LARRY BENSKY, after leaving the military upon completion of service, LARRY returned to the boyhood home where he was born and raised.

BENSKY became employed in the film industry enjoying a successful career in the editing of films and photos, he later moved on to become a car salesman as his silver tongue allowed for many Honda's to roll on the roads. Larry is happily married and spends much time watching his little grandkids. LARRY BENSKY became involved with his local Vietnam veteran's chapter in his community and volunteering his time in many of his chapter's events.

LARRY is indeed a special man, a good man, who has and continues to "give back" especially, regarding all other veterans. TOD MOROS is only a memory, still though, a real one.

BOBBY JOYCE, after leaving the military upon completion of his service returned to the boyhood home where he was born and raised. JOYCE joined his male family members on the docks of New York City performing long hours of hard work and still until this very day remains employed in his Union job capacity. Bobby always remained a generous individual sharing not only his hard earned wages with others,

BOB JOYCE is always present to lend a hand and of course his 'EAR.' Bobby is a bachelor after being married many years and splits time between New York and his other abode in North Carolina. BOBBY became involved with his local Vietnam veteran's chapter in his community volunteering his time in many of his chapter's events.

BOBBY is indeed a special man, a good man, who has and continues to "give back" especially, regarding all other veterans. TOD MOROS is only a memory, still though, a real one.

ROY BOY TSCHUDY, after leaving the military upon completion of service he returned to his boyhood home where he was born and raised. Roy became a member of the New York City POLICE DEPARTMENT, enjoying a twenty four year career in the Transit Division. ROY BOY and Lois were married in 1980, together raising their daughter Dawn now a married mother of three little boys and their son Andrew who is successful working in the entertainment industry.

ROY TSCHUDY became involved with his local Vietnam veteran's chapter in his community volunteering his time in many of his chapter's events. ROY is JUST a man, he tries to be good man, who has and continues to try to "give back" especially, regarding all other veterans. TOD MOROS is only a memory, still though, a real one.

CHAPTER 15

A few Of the Others

HOWARD GOLDIN, I would surmise that 'if' there was a Sergeant HOWARD GOLDIN he would have also returned home to his small town marry the love of his life and become a dad and probably a granddad also.

I would further 'guess' that HOWARD due to his leadership qualities would have become a police officer in his community and it would not surprise me one bit if he eventually during his career rose up through the ranks and became the CHIEF OF POLICE.

I could even envision a man as Howard continuing on as a wonderful humanitarian always helping veterans and children. Howard Goldin would most likely travel back to Vietnam every other year assisting in building clinics, an orphanage and a school or two. No, it would not surprise me in the least, 'IF' there was a real HOWARD.

PETER MARINO, most likely would have preferred to just be called 'Pete' by his friends. I would envision a nice easy going gent who would be more than happy to lend a helping hand to fellow service members; he would be the first in line to volunteer his time in aiding veteran causes. 'IF' there was a real PETER MARINO, it would be a privilege to know him.

TED GOODMAN, I can only think of a title that I would give to someone with the name GOODMAN that would be "A MENSCH." Everyone in life needs to have a friend who always has a smile on his face, always performs above and beyond whatever is needed.

Life would be great to have a "feel good" person, a man who can be uplifting when a friend is "down in the dumps." GOODMAN, what a perfect name for a GOOD MAN! 'IF' a Ted Goodman is a reality...

GLENN RIDDELL, just the name alone brings to mind a man who would be larger than life, a man who loved his country, his family and friends, a man who succeeded in every realm of his life. A man who served his country in uniform, a man who became powerful and influential in the political arena, only 'IF' there was a real GLENN RIDDELL, I would love to sit down with him and share a meal. Heck, we could even talk GIANT FOOTBALL. That would be nice.

CLIFF FROMM, 'if' there was indeed a real 'Cliffster' I would have loved to have met him and shared laughter and jokes with him. I would think of him as someone who is caring with a heart of gold.

I also would think a man like CLIFF would love to exercise and most probably would even run in a few marathon races. Why, I bet he probably would be a member of the

'Tribe' a nice Jewish boy. 'IF' there was a real CLIFFSTER, I think the world would be a better place.

JOHN LEIGHTON, Don't know why I would pick a name like that for a "fictional character" like all of the others being mentioned, just sounds like a good all American name to me. Saying that, he most likely would be an officer and I like the idea of him being a helicopter pilot.

'If' a man like JOHN LEIGHTON was a real pilot, I can only think of him being a leader of men who is honest and straightforward. For fun, I envision John with a funny little accent also.

ANTHONY LOMBARDI, what do you think that I could make up someone who is a pint sized hero? Really? How could someone so small in height and weight be a tremendous force against an enemy?

'IF' there was an Anthony, I would carry it further making him a tremendous athlete who especially loves baseball and umpiring. 'IF' there was a Lombardi I would also think he would lay down his life for veterans, a man who even ended with not one but two master degrees. 'IF' there really was a TONY LOMBARDI" I would be proud to have a man like that be a friend of mine.

PAUL MATTERN, 'IF' a man like Mattern existed, it would be sort of funny to have him be a real member of a BARBER SHOP QUARTET carrying around his little harmonica preparing his little ditties with a humdidlee hum deedo.

I would even venture to guess a man named PAUL MATTERN would end up working for the POSTAL

SERVICE so he would entertain those seeking to buy stamps. I would also think "IF" there was a Paul Mattern, he would be a loving husband, father, and granddad. A man who enjoys helping out other veterans, that's 'IF' Paul Mattern did exist.

WILLIAM 'WILL' WINTER, shouldn't every book contain a hero, real or imagined? Shouldn't there be a story regarding a special man" One man so special, so heroic, so brave, that reading about him and his exploits leaves the reader to conclude that a person like WILLIAM WINTER must be fiction? WILL WINTER who would be wounded two separate times serving his country in the jungles of Vietnam. WILL WINTER who would take only his knife edge with him venturing down into the depths of hell seeking an enemy?

More? You want more? I can take this beyond preposterous, WILL WINTER a young man who would return home to his Bronx roots and become a member of the New York POLICE DEPARTMENT. William Winter would once again heroically venture into the darkness of night, alone once more like many years after leaving the tunnels in Vietnam.

WILLIAM WINTER, foiling an armed robbery and once more being repaid for his bravery with a shotgun blast to his neck and face.

WILLIAM WINTER, WHO IS SELECTED AND ENTERED INTO THE ANNALS OF the 'N.Y.P.D.' POLICE OFFICER HISTORY AS A MEDAL OF HONOR RECIPIENT, 'IF' this was indeed the truth, you would be as lucky as I am to have him as your friend.

In total truth and with the utmost respect it is acknowledged that three men stated in the pages of this book and two of which were friends of mine did in fact make the ultimate sacrifice while in service to our Country in Vietnam.

SP4 JAMES PERRONE, REST IN PEACE.

SERGEANT D. STUDWAY, REST IN PEACE.

SP5 FRANK BEAVERS, REST IN PEACE.

*SERGEANT RICHARD RADOWICK, who gave his life as a civilian coming to the aid of an unknown female stranger in peril. Rest In Peace. P.S. Richard Radowick was both handsome and physically sound as described in this book, just like PERRONE, STUDWAY, and Beavers all good men.

*I would be remiss if I did not acknowledge MR. TOD MOROS. When the time comes we meet I would appreciate the warm embrace rather than a cold hand placed upon my shoulder. I mean, I'm just saying.

CHAPTER 16

TWISTS AND TURNS WITH A DASH OF IRONY

With respect to a few close friends who are Chapter 333 members of Vietnam veterans of America at their request I have excluded them from the book. I deeply appreciate their wish for privacy, I also acknowledge and understand for asking to be omitted and offer only gratitude for their service.

In a twist of irony, two members of the veterans "Nut Group" grew up together as good friends in the Bronx New York. We played baseball as teenagers on the same team and softball on the concrete field at P.S.96; we knew each other's entire family.

Down in Disneyland one of the attractions is filled with puppets from all over the world, hence, the song IT'S A SMALL WORLD, A SMALL WORLD AFTER ALL. Let me tell you how small this world really is! Stationed on the base camp named Can Tho located in the Mekong Delta 1968 Roy Boy (Me) was enroute down to the flight line. Passing a long row of tents in that vicinity I happened to glance towards my right when I recognized someone from the other side of the world. Well actually all I did see was a large nose protruding thru the tent flap, "Stop the truck" I yelled, "there is only one 'Schnoz' like that anywhere" I continued. Palmero!!! I called out, sure enough about another minute later the rest of John followed out from the tent.

Of course I'm just kidding, his nose isn't really that big but if this is a story that includes FACT, FICTION, and MYTH and if you knew John then it's easy to eliminate two of the three. I'm just saying.

All joking aside it was a wonderful feeling meeting up with my old boyhood pal, Johnny Palmero. The funny thing is when John spots me all he could say was "What are you doing here?" "Geez John, I think the same thing you are doing" was all I could muster in reply.

As I said, it was a great and warm feeling, kind of brought our home back to us a bit more closely. Whenever time would allow, the two of us would hang out for a bit and talk about our families, friends and times of innocence. We had our own "Olympic Day," the Britton street playground, "Zimmies" our neighborhood candy store, and a host of other remembrances. It was a good life, growing up in "Da" Bronx, growing up in the tall buildings known as the projects.

A few months after we reconnected, John caught the freedom bird back home to the world, we lost touch as often happens in life. Referring back to it's a small world, years later the two of us happen to meet again by chance in a small County of New York State named Rockland. Both of us long removed from the area we grew up and now both of us residing with families in Rockland, we remain close and good pals until this very day.

I was happy to learn that John did marry his girlfriend, the very pretty and sweet Susan also from our Bronx neighborhood. Together they have two beautiful girls who are both married with children of their own. Palmero used the G.I. Bill to further his education; he was always a smart kid and a good athlete.

As a member of our V.V.A. chapter we are fortunate to have him as our financial advisor "for life" who keeps close tabs on chapter funds. Even now, John is the same soft spoken modest person I remember from when we were kids. His hair may be a bit thinner, a few extra pounds around the middle, but the nose, ah the nose, oh well some things never do change!

THE ONE AND ONLY...BARNETT

"I want to lose a few pounds," those were the very first words I heard upon meeting Brian Barnett. We met at the local V.A. clinic for an orientation meeting along with a few other Vietnam veterans signing up for the health care system. This was the answer given by Brian to a doctor posing the question of "What goals would you like to achieve?"

This was at the beginning of a six week course set up by the veteran's administration as each of the eight other veterans also were requested to set a certain goal which they hoped to achieve. Week two of the training a V.A. clerical member followed up on the question posed the week earlier to each of us. When it was Barnett's turn to answer the question on goals and how much has he lost over the past week, Barnett answered the only way Barnett could, "Ya wanna know how much I lost? I lost SEVEN DAYS, that's what I lost!"

It was right then and there I knew that I was in for a treat, because it's not just WHAT Barnett has to say, it's HOW he say's it! Brian Barnett is a fake; he comes off loud and gruff, but in reality is nothing of the sort. Once you have the chance to know him as a friend the realization is that Brian is a big old Teddy Bear. Even though Barnett could not live down the embarrassment of admitting he voted for Obama, he repeatedly would say to us, "But not the second time," seeking forgiveness from a somewhat conservative group of veterans.

When it comes to engaging in Mother-In- Laws this is where Brian shines, "she wanted fresh rolls, so I head over to the A&P shopping store and get them as they come straight out of the oven, I bag a dozen and bring right on over to her," Brian relates to us all one day. "You think that she would say thank you or that she appreciates it? Not on your life!" After a squeeze or two of the rolls, "THESE ARE STORE ROLLS; I WANT RESTAURANT ROLLS, TAKE EM BACK."

Barnett's face becomes red and distorted in anger with his fist smacking up and down on a table which the rest of us are sitting next to, Barnett is now in full nut mode. Of course for the rest of us we are enjoying every minute of the show, I can't help but think to myself, hell, I would even pay to see this show again!

When Barnett is not throwing the old lady off of some imaginary building he then is in search of a "hit man," according to Barnett she plans on living another ninety years just to annoy him.

Living in area of the city that over the years has been in decline and crime infested, Barnett offers to move her from her apartment to a more safe and secure neighborhood closer to where Brian and his lovely wife reside, NO DICE! Brian tries to give the impression the mother-in-law is one big pain in the ass but he slips up on many occasions discussing her fully laying out that she is just a regular nice old Jewish grandmother. Brian Barnett without trying even a little makes comedians like Rodney Dangerfield, Henny Youngman, and Myron Cohen sound less funny.

Brian was in Vietnam or as he pronounces it, Vit, nam, was stationed somewhere on a plum farm in the middle of nowhere. "There were only two Jews in my company and we didn't crap from anybody, I was in Intel and would fly to other area bases delivering information." When Barnett finished his tour of duty along with his two year draft commitment he embarked on a myriad of jobs. Brian decided to become a Haberdasher, he would purchase dresses, shirts, pants and anything else that could humanly be worn then selling them for a profit. SUCH A DEAL!

Then there were the food trucks which Brian owned, he would sell sandwiches and drinks at many of the construction sites in New York City, winter or summer Brian would be on time with that little coin changer attached to his belt, ring ring.

Everyone would be better off in their lives if a person such as Brian Barnett entered into it. A little smile here, a big laugh there, Barnett is simply a good man who brings sunshine into this world.

COOKIES, I SMELL COOKIES

If any believe that the above phrase is attributed to the character on the PBS station Sesame Street Program "THE COOKIE MONSTER," they are wrong, pure and simple. The truth and fact of the matter this statement based on cookies has been established well before that program was born, in fact I would not doubt for a moment Sesame Street lifted it from our own BRUCE MCCLINTOCK.

The uncanny sense of smell which Bruce was born with is unmatched in the annals of time, if King Tutankhamen was buried with just one single cookie in the tombs of the Pharaohs Mcclintock would have found it along with any other archeology digs! The V.A. clinic where a few chapter members meet on a few occasions is on lock down status in the small kitchen area hidden in the rear. The administration is aware of the man named Mcclintock, aware of his magical skills in finding the slightest crumb. Round, square, rectangle, it is of little matter to Bruce what shape those morsels of sweet delectable's come in, what only matters is that they are cookies. The rumor has it that even if Bruce is blindfolded he will let all know what type of cookie is held before him and will even divulge if it is a chocolate chip type along with how many chips are in the cookie!

Bruce Mcclintock is one of the type of guys that if you know him for one hour, you have the feeling that you have known him all of your life. Cordial and friendly, always willing to lend a hand, Bruce can be counted on if need be. Bruce was born and raised in a small town and by his own admission was in "Hippie mode" for a while. One fine day Mcclintock received a letter from his Uncle, UNCLE SAM!

"GREETINGS", Bruce took in a long deep, deep breath and muttered what many others also have done, "Aww crap." Bruce said to the other veterans, "I just folded that letter up and put it in my pocket, no need to read the rest of it." Bruce was tickled pink to learn that he was assigned to the infantry and to make things even sweeter, that training would be in FORT POLK LOUISIANA! NOT!!!

Bruce relates to every person who has ever served in the United States Army, if given the opportunity to spend one year in Vietnam or one month in Fort Polk, NAM WINS HANDS DOWN! As bad as Polk was, the training received was as good a reason as any that Bruce was able to survive the war. Whatever Nam had in their jungles, Fort Polk could see it and raise the ante in its own jungle. Receiving his honorable discharge after spending his infantry tour in Vietnam along with the training at Polk, Bruce was a hardened veteran ready to handle any tough brutal job that presented itself. Using those skills and techniques Mcclintock took a special government job, a job where in all honesty many lives have been taken. Bruce Mcclintock a Nations hero, enlisted in the UNITED STATES POSTAL OFFICE! God love him, oh the bravery!

Bruce has been married to his beautiful Italian bride for near forty years, together he and Jackie have raised two daughters who have made them proud grandparents. Thank you Bruce for the friendship!

JAY 'BIRD' FINK

Jay is the oldest member of our chapter a few years past seventy now, Jay may be the oldest member but one thing is for sure…HE LOOKS IT! The 'Bird' is always complaining about memory loss. One of his more famous statements (Of which there are many) was made on week two of our Nam meetings, "I was a New York City fireman for over thirty years," pause, pause, pause, "Did I ever mention that I was a New York City fireman for over thirty years?"

Although Jay has a touch of forgetfulness all of the guys love him, 'Bird' brings his own unique distinctive personality that is unmatched. Jay enlisted in the United States Navy way back in 1960 when the ships were still made out of wood. He would have joined the Army but believed it would have been tougher than the Navy and it must have been so because Jaybird stayed in for nine years total.

On the second reenlistment Jay was shipped off to Vietnam, loading and unloading cargo and supplies while stationed in Da Nang. Jay 'Bird' Fink worked forklifts and heavy duty cranes ensuring all sorts of supplies reached the men in the front. One regret Jay always mentions is he helped unload barrels of Dioxins that was used for defoliation on jungle areas and dense areas where the enemy would hide.

"Agent Orange is something I can't get out of my mind," Jay has said many times it hurts him to think he was responsible about the after effects to veterans and others who have passed away from it. Jay has a great big warm heart; in that heart he also knows certain jobs were not always easy, the results of being in war. Jay does like to relive the notion of how he 'liberated' certain supplies which were intended only for the 'BRASS', not meant for the peons in the military.

Every now and then a pallet containing the finest alcoholic beverages would be unloaded by Jay and somehow it would mysteriously disappear finding its way to the sailors who worked the base. Jay believed that these special spirits should be shared among the real men in white caps and tight pants, not the ones who wore a chevron on their shoulders.

Being a good Bronx boy, 'Bird' would always whisper a "THANK YOU" to the brass whenever that mission was accomplished.

During our monthly chapter meetings Jay sits next to me on the left hand side, in truth I am happy that he does because Jay Fink is a good and close pal who always looks to help others whether a veteran or not. Jay can say things that are considered a little inappropriate now and then which in return may make meetings a little on the shaky side. Admittedly there are times 'Bird' is so comical one can be brought to tears, almost like instead of thinking to one self it is instead stated aloud.

Two years ago during our yearly Holiday Christmas/ Hanukah party a few of the guests were selected by random for the opportunity to pick a raffle ticket which would lead to a special gift prize. As luck would have it, one of the ladies chosen happened to be extremely attractive and blessed with very large and ample bosoms. When her name was announced she walked graciously up to the Dais (Most definitely appreciated by those of the male species) took the ticket in hand gave it a nice big kiss then placed that ticket right smack dab in the middle of her cleavage for good luck.

Silence, one could hear a pin drop and then a voice out of nowhere called out in a loud manner, the voice was unmistakable, undeniable; it was JAY 'Bird' FINK

"LUC-KEY... TIC-KEY!"

Those two simple words were drawn out in a thirty second interval; Jay spoke the truth on what every guy in the room was thinking to himself! Jay has run the Chapter 333 "BELLS AND WHISTLES" program for the past five plus years, selling items such as chapter T-Shirts, Golf Shirts, Sweatshirts also helping order silk jackets that bear the name of the veteran along with decals sewn on them.

Fund raising events in Malls and local sporting events assisting in finding younger veterans who would like to have their own special HAND CYCLE for either the physical rehabilitation to the body or the psychological aspect for the rehabilitation of the spirit, Jaybird Fink is always at hand to help.

Jay Fink is a pure hearted man without his help our special HAND CYCLE PROGRAM would not be successful to the degree it has become.

JON MASH

ZZZZZ, that describes our pal Jon Mash in a nut shell. Most people have a dog or a cat for their pet, Mash instead has a Tsetse fly! Well, at least the other veterans who know Jon think so; the man has fairy dust in his eyes 24/7 for crying out loud.

Jon is the chapters Rip Van Winkle of sorts who can fall fast asleep at the snap of a finger, a hypnotist's delight. Mash is a quiet man who enjoys the monthly chapter meetings and possesses a good knowledge of the stock market. Mash was drafted into the army while living in the Bronx N.Y. "The only time I have ever won anything for free in my entire life and it was a subway token," Jon likes to say, "The only problem was the token came with a letter which began, 'GREETINGS!'

Jon was sent to an infantry unit after spending his eight weeks of fun in the sun in basic training and then another lovely eight more weeks of enjoyment in A.I.T. before heading out to South East Asia. A few us have accepted the fact that Mash can get upset when or if addressing politics or politicians, to put it plainly, Jon does not have the kindest of words for either of them.

Taking a few civil service tests when he finally was honorably discharged from the army, Jon could have joined the police department or the fire department. Mash instead became a member of the city's Sanitation Department starting on the low end of the broom. Mash thought that he had seen everything by that time in his life, two years in the army along with the last year of it in the infantry located in the Central Highlands of Vietnam.

Booby traps in Nam and garbage cans in the Big Apple were almost equal in injury; dead animals to shitty diapers, dead human body parts were also on the menu. Jon said the rats that live in the tenements were plain old mean and were ready to do battle if approached trying to empty a can. Time to take a few promotional tests and leave that part of the job for another guy and that's what Mash did.

One promotion led to another and another and finally the last promotion, Borough Supervisor! Promotions are good for not only not having to perform the tasks as mentioned, the pay raise attached made for a very happy Jon Mash.

The pay was so good it helped put his son thru Medical school and become a Surgeon today, not to mention Jon's daughter graduate from a prestigious University as well. Jon Mash has done well for himself because of the work ethics he learned from his parents long ago. A regular guy who served his Country without complaint, a regular guy who married his love and raised two children who in return have helped so many others in their lives.

Tod Moros passed by Jon Mash and probably on a few other occasions as well. By doing so, Jon was and still is able to help others via Chapter 333 programs in place. Hey Mash, thanks for the friendship buddy.

JAMES P. PERRONE

Sunday March 12th 1967 most people enjoy the second half of their weekend in a host of different ways. For many of the Christian faith attending morning Church service along with exchanging handshakes and hugs is the norm. Others simply enjoy relaxing with their hometown newspaper catching up on current events and maybe a little town gossip as well. Visiting a relative and or a friend is on the agenda for some as well, its Sunday, a day to relax and give thanks.

Not so much for the men of the Second Platoon A Company, 2nd Battalion, 35th Infantry, 25th Inf. Division stationed in Pleiku Central Highlands Vietnam. Instead of getting ready to watch a spring training baseball game, sleeping in late from a late night out with friends or a date with a pretty young lass, these men, these soldiers, were on patrol in a jungle far away from home. Jim Perrone all six foot four inches tall who was born and raised in the Bronx New York could sense that this particular Sunday morning was going to be a little different than others. Jim has been in Nam for almost eight months, taller than most other men he usually volunteered to walk point on patrol. Eight months in a war zone participating in many fire fights is more than equal to a lifetime spent in freedom.

Jim always with a smile on his handsome face and a professionalism that belied his nineteen years of age took a bite out of a long stick of Italian Salami that was part of the care package his mom and family sent to him almost weekly. These food packages were filled with Italian delights which were shared by Jim equally among all of the platoon members. A few of the young soldiers never before had the taste of any of these delectable's, "What's a Cannoli?" asked one of the guys who was born and raised in the South. He soon found out and like anyone who has ever has tasted one, enjoyed it fully.

Jim Perrone along with his two younger brothers was born, raised and educated in the Bronx, one of the five Boroughs which in actuality make up the City of New York. Most folks think Manhattan inclusive of Broadway and Times Square is New York City when referred to; Manhattan is only one of the five Boroughs along with the Bronx, Brooklyn, Queens, and Staten Island. Reading a letter from home one day, Jim was aghast to learn that while he was away in the army, his parents uprooted from the Bronx and purchased a house in New Jersey.

New Jersey! Oh no, Wanaque Jersey c'mon. You can take the man out of the Bronx, but you can't take the Bronx out of the man, Jimmy is as Bronx as Bronx could be. Thinking about it almost whimsically, Jim would have to agree that New Jersey sure was more desirable than his current living area, the Central Highlands of Vietnam.

It was early that morning; Sunday March 12th James Perrone along with A Company operating alone in the deep jungle encountered a regimental sized unit of North Vietnamese Regulars. The enemy was well dug in and prepared for the unsuspecting smaller U.S. Army platoons. A battle ensued between the two armies, fierce fighting, loud gunfire exchanged, all unbeknownst to those back home reading their newspaper, visiting a friend or relative, relaxing and giving thanks.

One of the two platoons soon began to run low on ammunition with the need to re-supply fast, the platoon was in real danger of being completely wiped out by the larger enemy force. Aware that the end would soon be here for that platoon Jim Perrone along with another member volunteered to re-supply them with as much ammo they could possibly carry. Perrone was focused on only one thing; get that much needed help over to the other platoon as fast as his long legs would move.

Bandoliers strapped around his wide shoulders ammunition boxes in both hands, Perrone dodged enemy fire from all angles and sides. Taking quick cover behind a large stump of a onetime tree, Jim lifted his M-16 rifle and returned fire at two N.V.A. soldiers charging directly at him. No time to stop and dwell, his 16 returned over his soldier Perrone burst out from behind the tree stump running hard and fast, in a short time he was near the platoon in need of the supplies.

Once again Perrone came under intense heavy enemy fire forcing him into a small ground opening created by the battles mortar rounds. Sweating and breathing heavily, Jim Perrone was glad to discover another soldier jump into the crater with him as round after round pinned them down.

Taking a long deep breath, James Perrone inched up a little in the rough terrain to survey the area of fire, "Just a few more yards" Jim stated to the other soldier.

The enemy sniper was camouflaged, hiding in the jungle tree line fifty yards away observed the tall figure of an American soldier peering from a crater; taking aim he slowly squeezed the trigger. Jimmy locked eyes with the other soldier next to him, Tod Moros bent over extending both arms around Jim enveloping him in a peace he never felt before.

Death knows well the hearts of men, death is aware of goodness and kindness of men even in battles of war, death knew the soul of this soldier, son, and brother. As peace soon settled upon this nineteen year old hero he was calm and accepting of his time, words whispered into his ears left a lasting smile on the face of James Perrone,

"Greater love hath no man than this that a man lay down his life for his friends."May God bless and keep you always Jim. You're Friend, Roy

David Dunn
david.dunn@verizon.net
Platoon Leader
15295 SW Bull Mountain Road
Tigard, OR 97224 USA
"Head and Shoulders Above"

"Head and Shoulders Above" Specialist Fourth Class
(SP-4) James P. Perrone was a man and a soldier that truly
stood out from his peers. Though he actually was the tallest
man in A Company, 2nd Battalion 35th Infantry, Jim stood
"head and shoulders above" the rest of us not because of
his great physical height. He was "head and shoulders and
above" because of the immense strength and depth of his
character. Jim grew up in the Bronx and, as is typical with
so many New Yorkers, was quite animated and vocal. He
was also fiercely protective when it came to those members
of his "family", A Company and especially the 2nd Platoon.
Every man in the company knew him and respected him,
both as a soldier and as an individual. Even those few who
may not have liked him, gave him respect. In truth there
were very few that disliked Jim and those, only because
he constantly challenged them by his actions to be better
soldiers and individuals. Feeling a deep sense of patriotic
duty, Jim enlisted in the Army in 1966, after his family
moved from the city to Ringwood, New Jersey. His long time
Bronx buddy, Carl Schwarz, was drafted shortly thereafter
and both were sent to serve their country in Southeast Asia.
Carl was assigned to the Ninth Infantry Division in the
South while Jim went on to the Central Highlands settling
into the Second Platoon of A Company, 2nd Battalion, 35th
Infantry, 25th Inf. Division in Pleiku. Before departing the

Bronx, the friends made plans to get together during R & R later in their tours. Unfortunately Jim was not able to make that R & R rendezvous with Carl. While life in the Second Platoon was far from idyllic during those last days of 1966 and early months of 1967, there was a wonderfully pervasive sense of personal regard for one another. Though everyone seemed to contribute to that feeling in one way or another, it was Jim's contribution that was huge. Not only did he always carry considerably more than his share of the combat equipment load, he often volunteered to walk "point". Though his tall, lanky frame may have been a bit of a liability for his own personal safety, we all felt very comfortable while Jim was leading us through those thick jungles in the mountains of the Central Highlands. Jim truly approached his duty as a soldier with an extraordinary level of professionalism, particularly for a man of his age and experience. We always knew that if Jim said it was safe, it was. If he said there are NVA close, they were there. He had excellent powers of observation and paid attention to the smallest details. Though Jim carried out his soldiering duties as a true professional, he also had a fantastic sense of humor. Just listening to Jim engaged in an ordinary conversation with a buddy often brought smiles to the faces of those other listeners nearby. He had an uncanny ability, a gift really, to see and portray humor in nearly everything. He was a true delight to be around. Endowed with so many positive character traits, it is hard to pick the "one extra special" part of Jim's character. He often talked about home, his family and friends. He was also continually helping those around him in countless little ways. His generosity was truly extraordinary. While others may have hoarded bits of "care packages" from home, Jim always shared his "packs" with the platoon. To this day I can still taste the Italian Salami that his Mom would send him from time to time. To me though, it was his expression of deep love and heartfelt concern for the wellbeing of his family, both at home and his "adopted family", A Company. He was some kind of man and one that I will never, ever, forget. I had the honor of being Jim's Platoon Leader from December 1966 through March 12th, 1967. Early on that March day A Company, operating alone, encountered what the records say was a regimental sized unit of North Vietnamese Regulars. They were well dug in and prepared. Within a short period of time two A Company platoons became heavily engaged. It was not long before one platoon ran dangerously low on ammunition and sent out two men to affect a re-supply. I remember, as if it were yesterday, that when it was time to send the ammunition back to that heavily engaged platoon it was Jim that stepped up to me and said selflessly, "I'll go". Sadly the return trip proved deadly and all those brave men were either killed or wounded prior to reaching their objective. They were courageous men, selflessly giving of themselves in an attempt to help others. They were, and are, real heroes. Specialist Fourth Class James P. Perrone was a true patriot, a fine soldier and an outstanding human being. I know that all those he was around, so many lives, were enriched in such a wonderful way. I will be forever honored to have served with this fine young man. He was, and will forever be, "Head and Shoulders Above". David Dunn 2nd Lt., Second Platoon Leader A Company, 2nd Battalion, 35th Infantry, 25th Infantry Division December 1966 - May 1967

Tuesday, April 06, 2004

One of the last photos of my brother. Photo taken in June
of 1966 Sunday, September 08, 2002 Robert Perrone

HOWARD GOLDIN

"Son, you are one very fortunate soldier" Major John P. Collins stated to Howard Goldin as he bent over at the waist pinning a Purple Heart Medal on the wounded Sergeants upper right side chest while recuperating in a hospital bed. As the words were being spoken to Goldin the thought of being shot four times somehow did not give Howard much comfort. Smiling when seeing the perplexed look on Howards face the Major continued further, "What I am getting at Sarge is if you were not tended to as fast and as well by that medic you would have bled out in the field. Your medic saved your life son it's as plain and simple as that."

The Major quickly moved on to the next bed for the same protocol as he would do the same with the dozen or so others all laying in a hospital room located in Da Nang Vietnam. Still, Howard did not feel so lucky and thought the Major to be a little bit of an ass to even suggest taking four enemy rounds to his left leg was not that big of an issue.

Shifting uncomfortably in his hospital room bed with his leg elevated in a sling at a 45 degree angle, Goldin could not help but replay the attack on the platoon almost three weeks ago. Goldin's squad was caught just like the rest of the platoon; Howard allowed himself a small smile recalling the speed in which his squad reacted to the sudden attack. My team fought like the true warriors they are he thought to himself, at the same time Howard was engaging the enemy he continually barked commands out to his men, all were adhered to like clockwork.

This was not Goldin's and his squad's first rodeo, his team was well trained just the way a professional football team would have a game plan prepared. Teamwork that has been instilled since each soldier entered into boot camp, into A.I.T. and now in the fields of Nam kept them alive. One unit working like an entire hand, not one or two fingers separately, one hand delivering a mighty blow in the form of a fist, up yours Charlie!

"I got ya Sarge, yer gonna be fine the Beave is here to take care of you." Ahh, of course Frank Beavers, Goldin continued replaying the entire battle scene to him. Frank Beavers a nineteen year old medic who hailed from the tiny Town of Newhall in West Virginia was the main reason Howard Goldin was still in the land of the living. It first felt like I was punched in the leg and as I went down three more enemy rounds hit me through and through Goldin remembered. BURNING, the burning sensation arrived within seconds of hitting the earth, never felt anything so hot before in my life he kept on recounting.

Through all of the shouting and cursing that enveloped the scene, through all of the rounds exchanged between the N.V.A. and the platoon, throughout all of the madness of the battle, Goldin was alert and never more sharp minded as then. Frank Beavers despite the rage of battle all around managed to dress Goldin's wounds stop the bleeding completely and get him on a gurney out to a safe area. Giving the Sarge a pat on the back and his little goofy smile "I told ya I would take care of ya, I'll be see'in ya later buddy."

There was one particular soldier who stood out in Goldin's mind, a soldier who was familiar to him but Howard never did get his name. This one soldier alone was an incredible killing machine; he was laying waste to the

N.V.A. like nothing Howard had ever seen before. Goldin caught a glimpse of his face just as he was hit and going down, that soldier stopped his killing for a second and began to move towards Goldin. Then, out of nowhere, Frank Beavers appeared beginning his first aid on his Sergeant; Howard took note of the soldier returning to take lives.

Frank A. Beavers Branch of Service U.S. Army Rank SP5 can be found on Panel/Row: 39 E; 28. Frank Beavers nineteen years of age born May 13th 1948 was killed in action Feb. 14, 1968. Frank Beavers died attempting to save another wounded soldiers life, gone in a flash.

Valentine's Day is a day for lovers to be lovers, a day to kiss and hold hands, a day to whisper sweet nothings in the ear of the person you care for. Flowers and candy, cards and letters make for a lovely and sweet time of the year. May 13th, Valentine's Day will always be remembered with sadness by one Sergeant Howard Goldin who lost his friend that day at the tender age of nineteen. There was no cold hand of DEATH placed upon young Beavers shoulder that day of May 13th, knowing his great care and love for his 'Brothers', knowing the pure innocence of his soul, Frank Beavers took the hand of TOD MOROS and was given a private escort to the Lord.

Sergeant Howard Goldin

To the memory of Frank who died heroically at age 19.

January 14th 1969 the day after Sapper Attack.
Two Chinook helicopter's destroyed.

William Winter
U.S.M.C. "TUNNEL RAT"
Wounded in Action Two Purple Hearts
N.Y.P.D. Wounded in Action
MEDAL OF HONOR RECIPIENT.

Sergeant Tony Lombardi "Tunnel Rat"
Receiving the Silver Star.

Roy Boy First Day in Nam.

Sergeant Richard Radowick

L-R: Roy Tschudy 'Cliffster,' Fromm, Roger DuPont

Bruce Mcclintock
"Hiding his Cookies behind his back."

Bobby Joyce

'Captain' Glenn Riddell and Roy Tschudy

Lee Pelton

L-R: Jay 'Bird" Fink, John Palmero, Paul Mattern
Chapter 333 Volunteer Gabriella D'Amico

Ray Ray

Roy Boy Base Camp "Shit Burning Detail"

Top: Squad leaving for night perimeter guard duty;
Second: Roy Boy at the "Command Bunker"
Bottom: Roy Boy Base Camp Can Tho,
Roy Boy "Tent City"

Roy Boy

Captain John Leighton

Brian Barnett

Larry Bensky

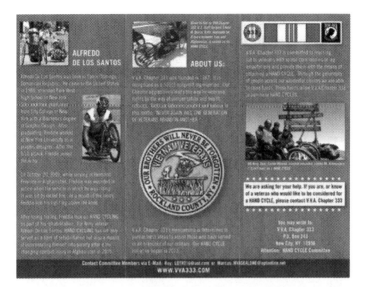

V.V.A. CHAPTER 333 located in Rockland County N.Y. continues on with an initiative that began in 2013. The members are continuously searching for fresh ideas to assist the community at large and especially those who have served in all branches of our military.

One of the many positive programs CHAPTER 333 has embarked on is donating special HANDCYCLES for Iraq/Afghanistan veterans with leg amputations and or spinal cord injuries. Via fundraising efforts, speaking engagements, and other forms of public awareness, a successful campaign has been implemented for assisting our "Brothers and Sisters" in need.

Inclusive with Chapter 333 members, are members of THE MILITARY ORDER OF THE PURPLE HEART. Specially designed Hand cycles have been donated to the Veterans hospital in Castle Point N.Y. along with the V.A. campus located in Montrose N.Y.

The cycles are used in the rehabilitation departments for dual use which is also for recreation purpose.

In addition to those donations of Hand cycles, CHAPTER 333 has been fortunate enough to purchase this item for other veterans with severe combat related injuries. Although under the banner of HAND CYCLES, we do not limit our offer of assistance to this single item. For instance, if a veteran would prefer a KAYAK to enjoy for a lake recreation we would consider this item also.

One of our cycle recipients Freddy De Los Santos is currently rated #1 in competitive racing with the Hand cycle purchased for him by Chapter 333. Veterans have expressed their deep appreciation for ownership of this item; we as a chapter have been "HUMBLED" to help them for both physical and mental recovery.

CHAPTER 333 continues to epitomize the Vietnam veterans Credo: "NEVER AGAIN WILL ONE GENERATION OF VETERANS ABANDON ANOTHER."

Please visit our Chapter website and view the many commitments this group of honorable men is involved with. www.vva333.com

Any who may wish to contribute to this most worthy cause may do so by sending a check for any amount desired to:VVA Chapter 333 P.O. Box#243 New City N.Y. 10956 * Please write "HANDCYCLE" on check.

NOTE: ANY AND ALL PROCEEDS FROM THE PURCHASE OF THIS BOOK ARE DIRECTED TO V.V.A. CHAPTER 333 HAND CYCLE PROGRAM.

DONATIONS MAY ALSO BE SENT TO:

V.V.A. CHAPTER 333
P.O.BOX 243 NEW CITY N.Y. 10956
(Please write: For HAND CYCLES on the check)
Said Chapter is a 501(C) request for tax exemption will be received upon request.
Please visit our website; www.vvachapter333.com
And, www.vethandcycle.com

Printed in the United States
By Bookmasters